Henry Gallant and the Warrior

H. Peter Alesso

HENRY GALLANT AND THE *WARRIOR*

This is a work of fiction. All characters
and events portrayed in this book are
fictional, and any resemblance to real
people or incidents is purely coincidental.

Copyright © 2015 H. Peter Alesso
All rights reserved.

Printed in the United States of America.

No part of this publication may be reproduced,
stored in a retrieval system, or transmitted,
in any form or by any means without prior
permission in writing from the publisher.

VSL Publications
Pleasanton, CA 94566
www.videosoftwarelab.com

Edition 1.00

ISBN-10: 1511691603
ISBN-13: 978-1511691604

Novels by H. Peter Alesso
www.hpeteralesso.com

THE HENRY GALLANT SAGA

Midshipman Henry Gallant in Space © 2013

Lieutenant Henry Gallant © 2014

Henry Gallant and the *Warrior* © 2015

∞

A warrior fights for his brothers.

His sacrifice makes him a hero.

1

GOING UP

Lieutenant Henry Gallant plodded along the cobblestone streets of New Annapolis—head down, mind racing . . .

My orders say take command of the Warrior *immediately . . . but no promotion . . . Why not?*

He pondered the possibilities, but he already knew the answer. Though he had steely gray eyes, a square jaw, and was taller than nearly everyone around him, what distinguished him most was not visible to the naked eye—he was a Natural—born without genetic engineering.

Is this my last chance to prove myself?

By the time he reached the space elevator, the welcoming breeze of the clear brisk morning had brightened his mood and he fell into line behind the shipyard personnel without complaint.

Looking up, he marveled: *That cable climbs into the clouds like an Indian rope trick.*

When it was his turn at last, the guard scanned his comm pin against the access manifest.

The portal light blinked red.

"Pardon, sir. Access denied," said the grim faced sentry.

"Call the officer of the guard," demanded Gallant.

The officer of the guard appeared, but was no more inclined to pass Gallant through than the sentry was. The guard touched the interface panel and made several more entries, but the portal continued to blink red.

"There's a hold on your access, sir."

Trouble already? Gallant thought. Then he asked, "A hold?"

"Yes, sir. Your clearance and authorization are in order, but SIA has placed a hold on your travel. They want you to report to SIA headquarters, A.S.A.P."

"I need to go to the shipyard and attend to important business before going to the Solar Intelligence Agency," clarified Gallant, but even as he said it, he knew it wouldn't help.

"Sorry, sir. Orders."

Gallant noticed the four gold stripes of a captain's sleeve. The officer was waiting to take the next elevator.

"Captain?" he said, hailing the man before he recognized him.

Captain Kenneth Caine of the *Repulse* marched to the guard post, frowning.

"What can I do for you, Gallant?"

Of all the luck, he thought. Caine was the last person he wanted to impose upon, but it was too late now.

Several uncomfortable moments passed with the three of them standing there—Caine, Gallant, and the officer of the guard—staring at each other, waiting for someone to break the silence.

Finally, Gallant addressed Caine: "Well, sir, I've received orders to take command of the *Warrior*, but apparently all the T's haven't been crossed and my shipyard access has a hold from SIA."

Caine's frown deepened.

Gallant turned to the officer of the guard and said, "Is it possible to allow me go to my ship and complete my business? I'll report to SIA immediately afterward."

The officer of the guard fidgeted and squirmed. He understandably did not like being placed in such a position while under the scrutiny of a full captain.

Caine shrugged.

Gallant was puzzled for a moment, wondering how to win Caine's support.

He tried the officer of the guard again, "Perhaps, you could send a message to SIA headquarters stating that you informed me of my requirement to report and that I agreed to attend this afternoon after I assume command of my ship. I'll initial it."

Caine nodded.

The guard brightened visibly. "That should be acceptable, sir." He made a few entries into his interface panel and the portal finally blinked green.

Gallant stepped through the gate and joined Caine. Together they walked to the elevator doors and mingled with the group waiting for the next available car.

"Thank you for your help, captain," said Gallant. "I'm sorry to have troubled you."

Caine merely nodded.

Unwilling to miss the opportunity to reconnect with his former commanding officer, Gallant asked, "How've you been, sir?"

Caine's frown returned. "Well, personally, it's been quite a trial . . ."

Gallant resisted the temptation to coax him onward.

After a minute, Caine revealed, "I lost a lot of shipmates during the last action." He sighed and took a moment to silently mourn their passing.

"I'm sorry, sir," said Gallant, who was sensitive to the prickling pain in Caine's voice.

Gallant then took a long look at the senior officer. He recalled a mental image of his former commanding officer—solidly built and squared shouldered with a crew-cut and a craggy face. In contrast, the man before him now was balding and flabby, with a puffy face and deep frown lines.

"Humph," grumbled Caine, recognizing Gallant's critical stare. "You've changed too. You're no longer the lanky callow midshipman who reported aboard the *Repulse* nearly five years ago."

"Thank you, sir," said Gallant, breaking into an appreciative smile.

Caine returned the smile and, warming to the conversation, he said, "We had a few good times back then—and a few victories as well—a good ship, a good crew."

A minute passed before Caine added, "As for the *Repulse*—she's suffered along with her crew . . . perhaps more than her fair share. As you know, she's has been in the forefront of battle since the beginning of the war, but when the Titans attacked Jupiter Station earlier this year, we took a terrible beating—along with the rest of the fleet."

Caine's face went blank for a few seconds as he relived the event.

"The Titans used nuclear weapons to bombard the colonies. The loss of life was staggering. Jupiter's moons are now lifeless, scorched rocks. The colonists fled on whatever transport they could find and they're now in the refugee camp on the outskirts of this city," said Caine. Then, trying to sound optimistic but unable to hide his concern, he added, "We gave the Titans some lumps as well. It'll be some time before they can trouble us on this side of the asteroid belt."

"So I understand, sir."

SWOOSH! BAM!

The elevator car doors opened with a loud bang.

Caine stepped inside. Gallant grabbed the strap and buckled himself into the adjacent acceleration couch.

A powerful engine pulled the glass-encased car along a ribbon cable anchored to the planet's surface and extended to the Mars space station in geostationary orbit. A balance of forces kept the cable under tension while the elevator ascended—gravity at the lower end and the centripetal force of the station at the upper end. The tiny vehicle accelerated swiftly to seven g's and reached orbit in less than ten minutes before braking to docking speed.

Gallant enjoyed a spectacular view as the car sped through the clouds. Below him was the receding raw red and brown landscape of Mars spread over the planet's curvature; above him was one of man's most ambitious modern structures; —a space station, replete with a shipyard that housed the newest space vessels under construction including Gallant's new command, the *Warrior*, as well as ships in need of repair, including the *Repulse*.

Gallant tried to pick out his minute ship against the much larger battle cruisers nested near it, but the rotation of the station hid it from view.

"*Repulse* is completing extensive repairs. She'll be back in action before long. I have a fierce loyalty to my ship and I know she'll acquit herself well, no matter what comes," said Caine.

"I'm sure she will, sir," said Gallant.

"I haven't congratulated you on your first command, yet" Caine said, extending his hand. "You've earned it."

"Thank you, sir," said Gallant, shaking hands, while a thought flashed through his mind,

If I earned command, why wasn't I promoted?

"Do you have any idea of your first assignment, yet?"

"No, sir. It could be almost anything," said Gallant, but he was thinking,

Probably involves the Warrior's *special capabilities.*

Caine said, "At least you'll get a chance to strike the enemy."

Gallant said, "We still know so little about the aliens' origins or intentions. Since they've taken Jupiter, they've expanded their bases from the satellites of the outer planets. They've also penetrated into the asteroids. That puts them in a position to launch raids here."

Caine said, "I once asked you, 'What's the single most important element in achieving victory in battle?'"

"Yes, sir, and my answer is the same: surprise."

"Yes," Caine said, "but to achieve surprise, it's essential for us to gather more intelligence."

"I agree, sir."

"Tell me, Gallant," Caine said, as he shifted position, "are you aware there are many people who hold you in contempt? They still doubt that a Natural can serve in the fleet."

Gallant grimaced. "I've always done my duty to the best of my ability, sir."

"And you have done admirably, from what I know of your actions, but that hasn't fazed some. I've heard little about your last mission."

"I can't discuss that mission, sir. It's been classified as need-to-know under a special compartment classification," said Gallant, as he thought,

I wish I could tell you about the AI berserker machine. I can only imagine what's in store for the Warrior.

"Nevertheless, I've heard that Anton Neumann was much praised for that mission. He was promoted to full commander and given the cruiser *Achilles*, though, I wouldn't be surprised if his father's influence played a role in that."

Gallant said nothing, but stared down at his shoes, *Neumann always wins.*

Caine grunted and then said, "Neither of us is in good standing with Anton's father."

Caine and Gallant had previously run afoul of Gerome Neumann, President of NNR, Shipping and Mining Inc., and an industrial and government powerbroker.

Gallant nodded.

Upon arriving at the space station platform, the elevator car doors opened automatically and once again banged loudly.

SWOOSH! BAM!

A long, enclosed tunnel formed the central core of the station with twenty-four perpendicular arms that served as docking piers. The tunnel featured many windows and access ports to reach the twenty-four ships that extended from the docking arms.

The two men chatted about the war news while they rode a tram along the tunnel causeway. Finally, Gallant left Caine at the *Repulse* and continued to his new command.

A swarm of workmen buzzed along the *Warrior's* scaffolding, cranes hauled machinery to and fro, and miscellaneous gear lay haphazardly about. An infinite amount of preparation was under way, servicing the ship in anticipation of her departure.

Gallant gaped . . . *There she is.*

He leaned forward to take in every line and aspect of the ship. Despite the distractions, he saw the ship as a thing of exquisite beauty.

The *Warrior* featured a smooth rocket shaped hull and while she was smaller than her battle cruiser neighbors, she weighed thirty-thousand tons with an overall length of one hundred and twenty meters and a beam of forty meters. She was designed with stealth capability so she emitted no detectable signals and remained invisible until her power supply required recharging. Her armament included a FASER cannon, several short range plasma weapons, and several laser cannons. She was equipped with an armor belt and force shield plus electronic warfare decoys and sensors. The ship's communications, navigation, FTL propulsion, and AI computer were all state-of-the-art. The crew of 126 officers and men, was highly trained and already on board. When the *Warrior* traveled through the unrelenting and unforgiving medium of space it would serve as the crew's heartfelt home.

The brief, relaxed sense of freedom that Gallant had enjoyed between deployments was coming to an end; his shoulders tightened in anticipation. He stepped onto the enclosed gangplank and saluted the flag that was displayed on the bow. Then he saluted the officer of the watch and asked, "Request permission to come aboard, sir?"

"Permission granted, sir," said Midshipman Gabriel in a gravelly voice that was totally at odds with his huge grin, dimpled cheeks, and boyish freckled face.

Was I ever that young? thought Gallant before he recalled he was only a few years older.

Boarding the ship, Gallant's eyes widened as he sought to drink everything in. He was impressed by the innovative technologies that had been freshly installed. The novelty of his role on this ship was not lost on him. Upon reaching the bridge, he ordered Gabriel to use the ship's public address system to call the crew to attention.

"All officers, report to the bridge!" Gabriel ordered. When the officers had gathered around him a minute later, he said, "All hands, attention!"

Drawn together on every deck, the crew stopped their work, came to attention, and listened.

Gallant recited his orders, "Pursuant to fleet orders, I, Lieutenant Henry Gallant, assume command of the United Planet ship *Warrior* on this date at the Mars' Space Station."

He continued reciting several more official paragraphs, but from that moment forward, the *Warrior* was a member of the United Planets' fleet and Gallant was officially her commanding officer.

With the formal requirements concluded, Gallant spoke over the address system: "At ease. Officers and crew of the *Warrior*, I'm proud to serve with you. I look forward to getting to know each one of you. For now, we must outfit this ship and prepare to do our job as part of the fleet. There are battles to be fought, a war to win, and the *Warrior* has a key role to play."

Satisfied with his brief statement, Gallant nodded to Gabriel.

Over the address system Gabriel announced, "Attention! All hands dismissed! Return to your regular duties."

Gallant stood before the officers on the bridge, addressed each by name and shook their hands, starting with the executive officer and then the department heads; operations, engineering, and weapons; followed by the junior officers. His first impression was that they were an enthusiastic and professional group.

"I will provide prioritized work items for each of you to address in the next few days as we prepare for our upcoming shakedown cruise. For now you can return to your duties. Thank you."

Gallant entered the Combat Information Center and pulled on a neural interface to the ship's AI. The dozens of delicate silicon probes touched his scalp at key points. It sensitively picked up wave patterns emanating from his thoughts and allowed him to communicate with the AI directly. Gallant formed a mental image of the *Warrior's* interior. While Gallant could use the interface for evaluating the ship's condition, the controls remained under manual control. He hashed out his priorities for his department heads to work on and sent them messages. He ordered them to address the myriad of items he had been mentally considering for hours. While he would have liked to have had a discussion with each officer individually, that would simply have to wait. It was time to get back to the space elevator. Gallant frowned in frustration at being pulled away by his appointment,

I'd better hustle to SIA.

2

SIA

The Solar Intelligence Agency thrived behind several layers of impenetrable security in a huge complex of interconnected, multistory buildings located on the outskirts of New Annapolis. The ultramodern buildings reflected a unique architecture of high arched ceilings and glass panels, looking for all intents and purposes, like any major corporate office rather than the most highly secretive and secure facility on the planet. However, to Gallant's discerning eye the ventilation shafts and power transformers on the periphery of the compound hinted that what was visible, was merely the tip of the iceberg—the most sensitive offices and analytical laboratories were buried deep underground.

Looking left and right from the main building's entrance, Gallant could see several nearby government facilities including the Space Academy and Fleet Command Headquarters.

As he entered SIA, a security guard scanned his comm pin and told him to pass. Another guard led Gallant to a conference room on the first floor. He had no sooner settled into a chair, when he heard a familiar female voice say, "Hello, Henry."

He glanced over his shoulder and recognized, Lieutenant Commander Julie Anne McCall, an SIA agent he had met at a debriefing some years earlier. Her eye-catching figure, striking blonde hair, and seductive smile were all part of the professional repertoire she occasionally employed to garner information from mesmerized individuals.

"Good afternoon, commander," Gallant said smiling, pleased to see a familiar face.

She returned his smile with a broader more intimate version of her own. She asked, "Would you like some coffee? You take cream and sugar, as I remember."

She swiped her comm pin over the table's automatic service dispenser and collected two cups of piping hot brew.

"Thank you," he said, taking a sip.

He found the quiet of the huge room bothersome: "Will there be others joining us?"

"No," she said as she strutted to a computer console.

"Is this about my last mission?" prodded Gallant.

"No."

Her monosyllabic responses puzzled him. She stood before the computer console and activated the large screen. When she entered her protocols, the screen displayed information marked Top Secret: ENIGMA."

She said, "Today, I'm going to be briefing you." She gave him a broad, enticing smile and added, "How do you like that?"

Gallant wasn't sure how to respond, so he remained silent.

"There's some essential information about the Titan's ability to communicate that Admiral Collingsworth wanted you to have before your mission."

"Mission?" Gallant asked in surprise, pushing his coffee cup away. "I haven't received an assignment yet. I'm in the middle of preparing my ship for a shakedown cruise this week."

"Don't worry; you'll get your orders after the shakedown cruise. For now, I'm going to enlighten you on the progress SIA has made in understanding Titan communications. You should be particularly interested because our success is directly attributable to the AI device you captured."

Gallant raised his eyebrows. He had assumed that nothing had come of the device he had taken from a Titan destroyer several years earlier.

"It took a couple of years of trial and error, but nine months ago, our agents were able to use a neural interface to connect to the Titan AI CPU device. Since then we've begun to understand their complex and involved communication methodology."

McCall examined Gallant's facial expression as she spoke, as if dissecting his reaction.

The enormity of the breakthrough wasn't lost on Gallant. After years of war, the United Planets had never been able to translate any message to or from the Titans.

"We've tried to capture another device," McCall said, "but the Titans continue to self-destruct their damaged ships. But, we had a stroke of luck about six months ago." Again she paused and studied Gallant. "During a skirmish between several ships, we succeeded in capturing two aliens alive."

Gallant couldn't have been more shocked. Since the start of the war, Titan soldiers had routinely committed suicide rather than submit to capture.

"How was that possible?"

"Like I said, we had a stroke of luck. The Titans were stunned unconscious by an internal ship explosion and we scooped them up before they knew what had happened. Since then, thanks to the captured AI device, we've been able to interrogate them using a neural interface."

Seeing Gallant's reaction, she added hurriedly, "Don't get too excited. Our agents have gotten only the most rudimentary idea of what they're actually saying. Our comprehension level has been minimal—kindergarten to first-grade level.

"But what we did discover was so striking that when we started to tell our superiors, they refused to accept our findings." She leaned back against the console table with her arms crossed over her chest. "Incredulity is often the first reaction to any paradigm-changing discovery. I faced similar skepticism when I discovered your talents several years ago."

Gallant refrained from showing any emotion, but he was excited about the possibilities.

"The nearest analogy I can make," continued McCall, "is that individual Titans are similar to what we would call an 'autistic savant.'"

She let that sink in for a moment before she showed a series of Top Secret displays on her panel. "Their communication is different from humans. It involves a combination of image, color, smell, sound, and touch—all synthesized in a different way from our speech and hearing. In addition, they can network with a few others to form a collective intelligence—a kind of 'conference call.' This autistic savant networking is a type of semi-telepathic super-intelligence."

"What do you mean by super-intelligence?" asked Gallant, sensing that she had revealed her central theme.

"I'll come to that in a minute," she said, tapping the console screen to change the page. "By using a neural interface that connects to both our AI system and to the alien AI device, we were able to understand a little of their thinking and communication process. For example, when I say the number forty-two, you think of an integer, written or spoken; one more than forty-one, one less than forty-three, or the product of twenty-one times two, and not much else."

Gallant noticed McCall's tendency to look up and to her left, as if concentrating on remembering something difficult, before once again gazing at him.

Her voice continued in a steady cadence as she ticked off her facts, "To a Titan an individual number such as forty-two has shape, color, smell, taste, and sound. Altogether this spectrum of sensory relationships represents a single unique concept—the number forty-two. When a Titan adds forty-two and forty-two, it gets two identical conceptual shapes that are merged to form something completely new and different with its own unique characteristics. All their numbers and words have a similar adaptation."

"Have you learned anything about how they're organized?"

"From our interrogations of the prisoners, we've learned that Titan society has a class structure," said McCall. "At the lowest level, the workers do the basic manual tasks of growing food and constructing buildings. The next level is the warrior class that serves in their armed forces. The third class runs their business and economy. Finally, the fourth, or ruling class, makes governing decisions. This last group is dominant while the lower classes are submissive."

"I see," said Gallant, looking from the view screen to McCall: "But why are you explaining all this to me?"

McCall slid closer to Gallant and gently touched his arm: "I would have thought you might have guessed by now. We'd like you to try to talk to the prisoners and see what more you can discover."

"Why me?" asked Gallant, distracted by her nearness, wondering if there was a hidden agenda.

Taking a step away, McCall said, "Our current effort to improve human intelligence through genetic engineering will take generations—and genetic modifications are not foolproof—you're evidence of that. As the beneficiary of a unique mutation, you are more talented at neural interfacing with AI than any of our best genetically modified officers. And your experience with the berserker AI at Tau Ceti was further validation of that point."

"But your officers were able to make some progress, weren't they?"

"Yes."

McCall hesitated before expanding, "Consider the possibility that someday soon, there may be an intelligence explosion. It might come from either biologically enhanced humans, or smarter AIs." She paused again before adding, "Machines that could mimic human common sense along with the ability to learn, reason, and solve complex challenges have been anticipated since the dawn of computers. But human level intelligence is not the ultimate goal—superhuman machine intelligence is. The capacity to radically outperform the best of today's human minds is called super-intelligence, whether performed by machine, or a modified human."

"And now you're defining our struggle against the Titans as a contest to achieve super-intelligence?"

"Yes, to some extent. It was already started in the twenty-first century when humans added significant cognitive and physical enhancements through genetic engineering.

Our ability to use the neural interface to connect with an AI is a product of that effort. But, even then, we feared that machine super-intelligence would arrive first."

"But you've found that things haven't gone as you anticipated," prodded Gallant.

His comment scored high on her emotional Richter scale; she leaned over him and brought her face close to his, expelling her warm breath into his face. She shook her head. With gritted teeth she admitted, "No, they haven't. First, you turned up—a gifted natural-selection mutation. You surprised us all."

Feeling like a bug under a magnifying glass, he sat stone-faced and was beginning to wonder if her true intent was to brief him or to evaluate him under this new paradigm.

"Surprised, or embarrassed?" he asked.

McCall backed away and instead of answering him, she continued; "Now we're confronted by autistic savant aliens capable of challenging our thinking even further."

Anticipating her intentions, Gallant suggested, "Let me try to communicate with the prisoners."

McCall waggled her finger at Gallant and said, "Follow me."

When they reached the seventh subbasement, McCall showed Gallant a well-equipped laboratory.

Afterwards, Gallant would recall his mixed emotions on first seeing the slight figures of the prisoners. They were held under restraints in two separate glass-paneled cells. Very thin and frail, the methane-breathing aliens had no hair or markings on their grayish skin. Their violet and cobalt eyes were iridescent and reminded him of death.

McCall stood back and let Gallant proceed to interrogate the aliens. Using an AI neural interface, he was able to "see" the visual representations of the individual Titan's thoughts and ideas, and then compare them to the database that SIA had accumulated. His mental presence introduced dramatic turmoil in the prisoners' behavior.

Slowly Gallant learned. He began by visualizing individual numbers as smooth and round shapes as if they were pebbles on the beach. The most beautiful were prime numbers which held outstanding qualities of shape, color, and texture. Soon numbers were flashing before his eyes. Words followed. The landscape of Gallant's mind found rough and irregular patterns of sensual color and perplexing images he tried to understand. After several hours, he was able to translate a few Titan concepts—to a limited degree. Before the end of the day, he was able to translate more of what the interface presented to him into complete concepts.

The Titan prisoners attempted to conceal their thoughts from him, but their natural instinct for networking allowed Gallant to eavesdrop on the innermost secrets exchanged between them.

Upon finishing for the day, he was still unsure if he were a part of the SIA's Titan interrogation team, or of SIA's super-intelligence research.

Either way, he made one startling discovery.

He told McCall, "The Titans are intent on occupying the entire Solar System, even if it means the genocide of the human race."

It was his turn to watch her reaction. He thought,

That should focus your attention back onto the prisoners—instead of me.

3

THE WARRIOR

"Request permission to get underway, sir?"

The booming baritone voice of his executive officer, Lieutenant John Roberts, brought Gallant's wandering attention back to the bridge of the *Warrior*.

Even though Gallant had met the man only a week earlier, he had already formed a favorable opinion of him. Roberts had a lean smooth face, auburn brown hair, and was of average height with a solid, but unremarkable build. In his mid-twenties, and only a year or two older than Gallant, he looked more mature and personable than the years suggested—a characteristic Gallant envied.

Putting aside his own aspirations to drive the *Warrior* on her maiden shakedown cruise, Gallant let Roberts take command of the maneuvering watch for the ship's departure from Mars Station. As XO, Roberts was responsible to the captain for the ship's overall performance and the conduct of its crew, but Gallant was anxious to gauge the man's ship handling instincts as much as he wanted to measure the *Warrior's* performance.

"Maneuvering watch is set. All stations report manned and ready, sir," said Chief Howard.

"Very well," said Roberts. He stepped up to the command deck and took the seat beside the captain.

Roberts ordered, "Engineering, bridge; standby to answer all bells."

"Bridge, engineering; ready to answer all bells, sir," came the response.

"Chief of the watch, release grappling magnets," said Roberts.

Seated in front of a master valve control panel on the port side of the bridge, Chief Howard said, "Aye aye, sir." A moment later, the grappling status lights shifted from red to green. "Green board, sir."

"Helm, thrusters ahead slow," said Roberts to the helmsman a few meters in front of him.

°"Aye aye, sir," responded the helmsman. "Thrusters, answering ahead slow—ten meters per second and increasing, sir."

The panoramic view on the screen at the front of the bridge allowed Gallant to observe the ship's progress. The most dangerous time for a ship was during maneuvers when leaving or returning to dock at a space station.

"Navigation, plot a course to our designated operating area," said Gallant. The shakedown drills and tests were to be conducted in a portion of space about ten million kilometers from Mars, away from the normal shipping lanes.

"Aye aye, sir. Course 186, mark two, sir," said the navigation station.

"Mr. Roberts, set course 186, mark two," said Gallant.

"Aye aye, sir," responded Roberts. Then he ordered, "Helm, engage sublight engines, ahead slow, come port five degrees. Set course 186, mark two."

"Aye aye, sir."

"The ship is on course, sir," reported Roberts.

"Very well, Mr. Roberts." Gallant was satisfied with his XO's ship-handling skills, but felt no need to compliment him for what was a standard procedure. It was his intention to give all his officers every opportunity to display their skills and develop their expertise under his guidance.

The *Warrior* was the first stealth FTL ship to be constructed by the United Planets, and though it was only a diminutive sloop, it was equipped with the most innovative technology, shields, weapons, and engines available. It had an antimatter fusion sublight engine and a dark matter FTL drive. It was designed specifically to conduct clandestine sabotage and spy operations. Though its crew members hadn't worked together before, they were a collection of talented technicians and engineers.

Just one week earlier, Gallant had been appointed captain pro temp; though he remained puzzled about the temporary status.

Listening to the growing bridge chatter, Gallant relaxed as the ship settled into a comfortable routine. He kept his own internal dialog . . .

It's up to me to shape the character of this ship and crew.

Steadily, the *Warrior* accelerated, moving farther and farther away from Mars.

"Sensors, report!" demanded Gallant.

"Mars Station falling astern, shipping lanes clear, no obstructions ahead, sir," reported the sensor tech.

"Very well," said Gallant.

The forward viewport verified a clear path ahead.

On the busy bridge, Midshipman Gabriel was one of those vying for Gallant's attention. He was the youngest member of the 126 person crew. He was quick witted and had a disarming grin with dimples to match. In addition, he had a habit of wrinkling his nose when he laughed which drew attention to him. As tradition dictated, Gallant had assigned the most junior officer to head the communications division.

As communications officer, Gabriel handed Gallant a message tablet with clearance instructions from the shipyard supervisor verifying their exit from port and authorizing further operations. Scanning it, Gallant checked off his receipt. He glanced around the bridge at the various consoles to verify that all conditions were satisfactory.

"Mr. Roberts," said Gallant.

"Sir?"

"You may dismiss the maneuvering watch and set normal cruising watch when you think appropriate."

"Aye aye, sir."

"Navigation, how long until we reach our operating area?" asked Gallant.

"Approximately four hours, sir."

"Very well."

Gallant was satisfied that everything was in order, and it dawned on him that it would be appropriate for him to walk through the ship to see how the crew was reacting.

"Mr. Roberts, I'm going on a brief walk-through of engineering."

"Yes, sir," said Roberts. "Sir, navigation shows some shipping may eventually encroach on our track. Request permission to maneuver as required?"

Gallant looked over the plot and said, "Permission granted."

With that, he vacated his command chair and left the bridge, heading first for his cabin a dozen steps away. The cabin served alternatively as a sanctuary and an isolation cell with a bed, a desk, and a single cabinet. Looking around, he remembered the miniature quarters he had as a midshipman. These accommodations were almost as small. Conditions for his officers and crew were even tighter, and some of the crew had to "hot bunk"—one crew member used the bunk while another was on duty.

Over the ship's address system he heard, "Now set the normal cruising watch; section one. Now set the normal cruising watch; section one."

Gallant wandered through the *Warrior*. The ship was divided into three main compartments: bow, mid-ship, and aft. The bow compartment housed the ship's sensor arrays, its weapons systems, and the stealth technology. The mid-ship compartment, also called the operations compartment, was composed of three decks. It included the bridge and CIC on the first deck, the wardroom on the second deck, and the crew's living quarters on the third deck. The aft compartment housed the engineering spaces including the sub-light and FTL engines as well as the hangar bay. Running and maintaining an advanced ship was a huge job for such a small crew. Considerable automation was used throughout the ship, but controls could not be reliably left to AI and machines alone. It still required a human touch and human understanding.

"Good morning, sir," said Chief Howard. Benjamin Howard was a seasoned veteran and the CPO of engineering. He was the only person aboard the *Warrior* with whom Gallant had previously served. While his brown-gray hair was thinning and he sported a slight potbelly, he wore an immaculate uniform. The jaunty way he walked had been developed while in many different gravitational environments.

"Good morning, chief. How's your engine room?"

"Well," Chief Howard said, "over the past week, just when I got everything exactly the way I like it, the XO would hold a surprise inspection and make me 'clean it up' all over again."

Gallant smiled and said, "I'm sure it will find its way back to your satisfaction before long."

"It's hard to admit," Chief Howard said, "but I'm secretly glad the XO pays such close attention to detail. He might catch something I've missed."

Gallant said, "That's his job, but I doubt he'll discover that you've missed a trick."

Howard nodded: "Thank you, sir. Engineering is gathering information on our initial startup now, but the issues seem to be mostly minor adjustments. A few pieces of equipment have failed, but they're easily replaced."

"Good. Good."

Gallant returned to the bridge in time to see the ship reach her destination. The crew was chatting, anxious to begin the *Warrior's* first drills.

"Request permission to conduct scheduled exercises, sir," asked Roberts.

"Permission granted," said Gallant.

Roberts ordered, "Helm, ahead, one third."

The term 'shakedown cruise' started with seagoing ships conducting sea trials to shake-down a new ship's many fixtures and fittings. It was a test of performance including speed trials, crash stops, endurance, and maneuverability. For the *Warrior,* it was also necessary to test the advanced on-board technology. There were three key pieces of equipment that needed testing: first, the sublight engines would require maneuvering drills; second, the stealth cloaking system would be tried and evaluated; and third, the weapon systems, including the FASER, laser, plasma, and antimissile batteries, would require target practice.

Having reached the operational area, the *Warrior* began maneuvering exercises. Day one of the shakedown cruise started with testing the sublight engine with man-overboard, loss of steering, loss of propulsion, loss of reactor control, fire, and hull rupture drills.

The sublight fusion engine consisted of simple antimatter fusion reactors using an ordinary plasma containment field to drive the ship during normal interplanetary travel. The antimatter engines shot antiprotons into the nucleus of deuterium atoms, which caused a release of fusion energy. The antiprotons had to be isolated in plasma bottles surrounded by powerful, superconducting magnetic coils.

The initial drills involved simple changes in course and speed under emergency conditions. After several hours, Gallant allowed the second series of more stressful tests to begin, including depressurizing and pressurizing of compartments to check the hull integrity of the ship.

They were not able to test the FTL drive while they were in the inner portion of the Solar System, so they ran performance and functional tests on its associated equipment. They intended to conduct an FTL test once the ship had traveled to the outer planets at the end of their mission.

Toward the end of the day, they evaluated the stealth technology and the *Warrior's* ability to penetrate enemy defenses and evade detection. A drone was deployed with a sensor array to find and track the *Warrior* when she was in stealth mode. The stealth technology was based upon a dark matter superconductor that created a confinement field to cloak the ship. It required several minutes to energize and activate. The time required to enter and leave stealth mode was noted.

Finally, they began exercising the two small craft on board, an ordinary one-man Hummingbird flyer and a super-stealthy two-man Wasp.

Roberts had scheduled a full day of activities and the crew was exhausted by its end. The first day's activities ended satisfactorily. They acquired a great deal of information about the ships performance and the crew's ability to handle it. When they were completed, Roberts turned to face his commanding officer.

Gallant said, "I would like to have officer's call in the wardroom this evening to go over plans for tomorrow."

"Aye aye, sir" Roberts responded.

4

THE WARRIORS

Located aft of the officers' quarters, the wardroom of the *Warrior* was designed to accommodate the majority of the ship's officers in one sitting. On the wall over the head of the central table was the ship's plaque inscribed with a figure of the ship and the designation UP *Warrior* SS 519.

Gallant entered the crowded wardroom and took his seat at the head of the table. He said in a distracted manner, "At ease, gentlemen. Carry on while I get my notes organized."

He settled into his chair and tapped his tablet in apparent concentration but all the while quietly observing his officers.

Roberts was seated between Lieutenant Andrew Clay, the weapons officer, and Lieutenant Thomas Walker, the ship's engineer. Each had a mug of coffee in one hand and a tablet in the other. They were diligently looking over their department's list of problems while sipping the piping hot beverage.

Sitting at the foot of the table was young, innocent-looking Midshipman Michael Gabriel.

"Go on, Gabriel," said Roberts. "You were telling us about your decision to attend the academy."

With a lively and good-natured grin, Gabriel said, "I was born in New Annapolis, so I was exposed to the traditions and values of the academy while I was growing up. I attended parades, award ceremonies, and some sporting events. When the midshipmen were on town liberty, they would tell me wild tales that I only half believed, but they made me yearn to be part of their world. When I became eligible, it seemed only natural to apply to the academy."

He blushed before continuing: "The first year was challenging, as you know, but I thoroughly enjoyed my second year, and I was thrilled when my first deployment orders placed me on the *Warrior*. This is my first time away from home, and I hope to have some great stories of my own to tell when I return."

There were a few good-natured chuckles around the table.

Clay chortled, his long legs barely fitting under the table. He pulled at his thick black hair hanging slightly over his ears. "I graduated from the academy in '67," he said. "The nitty-gritty of that experience was that I learned to hate getting up at the crack of dawn."

Again the officers guffawed.

"If you had been born on a farm like me," said Roberts, "you wouldn't have suffered from that problem."

Walker scoffed. "When I was growing up, I thought I'd be brave and bold like the knights of Camelot," he laughed. "It seems childish now, but I was worried I might not be tough enough. I sometimes got into fights at the academy, though when I think back on them, I can never remember the reason they started." Of average height and slightly overweight, Walker had a pleasant voice to match his dry sense of humor.

Gallant wretched his mind away from and the chatter and focused once more on the shakedown cruise: "Let's discuss the *Warrior's* performance. Gentlemen, please look at your tablets and find the issue list I've sent to your respective departments."

Each officer had a long list of mechanical or electrical failures they were working to correct. The maneuvering drills had gone reasonably well, and the engines were close to meeting specs. Some of the stress tests had revealed deficiencies that would need recalibration at the shipyard.

Gallant ran through the reactions of his officers during the day's drills to see if there were faults he needed to correct, but failing to identify anything significant, he resumed his scheduling of the next day's activities.

When they were finished, a virtual readout of priorities showed up on their screen, and Roberts put together a memo to be distributed throughout the ship to give the crew a heads up for what was to come the next day.

Gallant asked, "Have we missed anything?"

"We need to make adjustments on some equipment in engineering and the sensor systems need to be realigned. I'll take care of those, sir," said Roberts.

"Good. I think we've covered everything. I'll leave the details in your hands."

"Very good, sir," said Roberts.

※

The next day, Gallant sat in his command chair reviewing the *Warrior's* sleek characteristics and unique features. Her sophisticated weapons technology was to be the focus of the day's activities. The ship's heavy caliber weapon was the FASER that was capable of seriously damaging a battle cruise with one hit. The four laser cannons and four plasma weapons were lighter caliber for close-range fire support.

Just as the name LASER stands for Light Amplification by Stimulated Emission of Radiation, FASER stands for Fission Amplification by Stimulated Emission of Radiation. A laser works by pulsing light through a crystal in such a way that the crystal releases a flood of identical electromagnetic waves simultaneously. The FASER cannon pulses light through a block of crystalline Uranium-235 so that all the atoms fission simultaneously to produce a beam of highly focused energy.

"Skipper," Roberts said, "I'd like to suggest that we hold a shooting competition. We could award a marksmanship badge to the battery with the best firing score."

Gallant smiled and said, "I like that idea, XO. Set it up. A little competition would be a great way to stimulate some friendly rivalry."

When weapons' personnel were stationed, the day's drills began.

"Prepare to launch the target drone," said Gallant.

"Aye aye, sir," said Chief Howard at the bridge control console. A remote control drone was released. It pulled a large metal sheet that acted as a target.

As the drone began to tow the target, the FASER fired a direct hit, vaporizing it.

They brought the drone back and added another metal sheet.

Next they fired the AMM-3 Mongoose antimissile missile. A drone simulated an enemy missile, and the Mongoose's on-board AI system directed it to the target, despite the drone's countermeasures.

This was followed by a series of plasma and laser target exercises until suddenly a loud alarm sounded . . .

CLANG! CLANG! CLANG!

A series of emergency messages blared from the AI system: "Explosion in the bow compartment! Loss of air in the bow compartment! Fire in the bow compartment! Damage control party, proceed immediately to the casualty!"

The ship's emergency teams sprang into action.

Gallant turned to the junior officer of the watch: "Mr. Gabriel, take charge of the damage control party in the forward weapons compartment. Report the status of the casualty as soon as you get there."

"Aye aye, sir."

A few minutes later, Gabriel reported, "Bridge, DC; I've reached the bow compartment and my team is donning their fire protective gear and breathing apparatuses. Chief Howard has reported that the team is ready. We are entering the compartment."

Gallant was gratified to hear Gabriel speak in a relaxed, confident voice.

The overhead fire suppressant system spewed out chemical material to dampen the fire while automatic hatch closures isolated various parts of the compartment to prevent widespread decompression from any hull breech.

Gabriel and the DC team entered the compartment and were immediately engulfed in smoke.

"Kill all the electrical panels on the port side!" Gabriel ordered, "Shut all the port side isolation valves!" He evacuated everyone else in the compartment and let the casualty team deal with the injured.

After several minutes of hazardous work, Gabriel reported, "Bridge, DC; the fire is out. Two men have been evacuated to sick bay with burns and smoke inhalation. One of the men is Lieutenant Clay."

With the fire extinguished, Gabriel went on to deal with the leaking rupture from one hull discharge valve. Chief Howard was able to apply a temporary patch, and the compartment pressure was restored to standard density.

Gabriel returned to the bridge where Gallant acknowledged his performance with a frank, "Well done."

Later in the wardroom, the officers jostled Gabriel good-naturedly. His popularity was due as much to his personality as to his actions that day.

The next day Gallant convened a board of inquiry in the wardroom. He sat at the head of the long wardroom table flanked on either side by the XO and the ship's engineer. Midshipman Gabriel and Chief Howard were seated along the side of the table. They were to be called as witnesses.

At the foot of the table, Lieutenant Clay stood with his arm bandaged. His grimace was as much from embarrassment as from pain.

"This inquiry is to investigate the explosion that occurred in the bow compartment yesterday," Gallant began. "It will be used as the basis of our accident report to Fleet Command." He paused and looked around the room. Then he said, "Lieutenant Clay, please explain how the explosion occurred."

Clay frowned and said, "I was working with a tech on plasma battery number one. The weapon had misfired during target practice, and we were trying to determine the cause of the malfunction. While we were conducting signal transmission tests within the trigger circuit, a fire was started by a short in a faulty electro-pneumatic switch on the plasma charging tank. The tech was overcome by fumes." He stopped and rubbed his bandaged arm. He looked confused.

Gallant waited patiently, all the while evaluating Clay's behavior.

After a moment, Clay recovered his focus and continued, "I immediately hit the emergency alarm, and the fire suppressant chemical flooded the area, but it wasn't quick enough to stop a fuel tank from exploding and sending metal fragments through the bulkhead and surrounding pipes. The shards ruptured a hull discharge pipe that leaked oxygen out of the ship. At no time was the hull itself penetrated. The hull's armor is much tougher than that."

"Why didn't you pre-station a damage control team before working on such a dangerous repair?" Gallant asked.

Clay looked angry and barked, "I didn't want to slow down the exercises for what looked like a quick fix."

Gallant glared at him and Clay continued, "It shouldn't have been a problem if the shipyard had installed and calibrated the equipment properly."

Gallant was quiet for several minutes while he considered the possibility of other shipyard failures that could plague his ship. "Please let the record show that the injured tech will make a full recovery in a few days and that Lieutenant Clay suffered burns on his left arm that will leave him on restricted duty for at least a week."

Clay shifted his feet slightly but remained silent.

Gabriel and Howard reported on their actions during the damage control team's effort to put out the fire and stop the air leak.

Gallant conferred with the XO and then reported the inquiry's findings: "Mr. Clay, for failure to follow safe repair procedure, you will receive a Letter of Reprimand in your file. In addition, you will be required to undergo additional training on correct repair and maintenance requirements while working on live weapons."

"Yes, sir," said a distraught Clay.

"I will complete my accident report for Fleet Command this evening. That's all. This board of inquiry is closed."

Gallant left the wardroom unhappy about issuing a letter of reprimand but feeling greatly relieved that the injured men would recover. He also made note of the dark cloud on Clay's face.

Gallant sent an accident report to UP command. That night the damaged *Warrior* left her operating area and headed back to Mars Station. When she returned, he prepared a list of needed repairs and upgrades. Once the *Warrior* returned to its berth in the shipyard, a work schedule was set up, but before anything was accomplished, Gallant said, "Roberts, I'm going planet-side. I won't be available until tomorrow."

Roberts' face showed his surprise that the captain would leave with so much activity about to begin on the *Warrior*, but Gallant just shrugged as he thought,

I have a very personal matter to attend to.

5

VOWS

It wasn't that Kelsey Mitchel was stunningly beautiful, though her smooth white skin and dazzling green eyes complemented the hazelnut hair that cascaded down her shoulders, nor was her poise and demeanor overtly eye-catching, though her manner was such that you would be curiously drawn to her. No, what seemed to attract the most attention was her bubbling personality. Her heritage and genetic birthright were clearly superior and set her apart from the women in the church crowding around her. And on this special day, her veil and flowing white gown doubly marked her. She was a mere twenty-three, and she radiated an appealing youthful vitality. You could imagine that once she captured a man's attention, he would find her hard to let go, let alone be willing to give her up entirely. But that was not the end of her allure, for upon knowing her, you discovered her intelligence, courage, and perseverance. She was a unique and desirable woman—an outstanding exemplar of her family and the times in which she lived—a woman any man would be honored to marry.

"If anyone can show just cause why this man and this woman should not be joined in holy matrimony," the minister proclaimed, "speak now or forever hold your peace."

This was the final opportunity for Gallant to intervene in an event that he thought was misguided. He should declare his objection to a union that could lead to a lifetime of regret.

"Do you take this man to be your husband? To love, honor, and keep him in sickness and in health, forsaking all others as long as you both shall live?" asked the minister.

"I do," said the bride.

Gallant stood like a statue in his blue service dress uniform.

Only a short distance away, dressed in her flowing white bridal gown, Kelsey seemed happy—or was she merely resigned?

"Do you take this woman to be your wife? To . . ."

Gallant had stopped listening. He couldn't bring himself to shatter her day.

". . . forsaking all others as long as you both shall live?" concluded the minister.

"I do," said Anton Neumann.

As Kelsey and Anton completed their marriage vows, Gallant continued to watch silently from a few pews away. The ornate cathedral was packed with stylishly dressed people, all eager to bear witness to the finale of the ceremony. The stained glass windows filtered multicolored streams of light into the traditional wedding ceremony, accentuating the variety of the participants. The people leaned forward in their seats and focused on the couple at the head of the chapel.

"I now pronounce you husband and wife."

Having borne witness to the ceremony, Gallant thought, *There, that's done. There's no going back.*

He wondered if, in time, he would come to regret his decision to remain silent. He sought comfort in the thought that despite his reservations, the couple might yet find their way together. How could he know?

He watched Kelsey and Anton embrace and kiss and then wave to the spectators. The couple then strolled along the pews to the front of the church.

As the congregation slowly followed to offer their good wishes, Gallant trailed in their wake. When he was a few people back in the receiving line, he saw Kelsey recognize him. Emotions passed over her face, but he couldn't ascertain their meaning.

"Congratulations," said Gallant while shaking the groom's hand. Neumann's deadpan blue eyes stared at Gallant for a second before he responded with a matter-of-fact "Thank you," and nothing more.

Gallant stepped toward Kelsey and was instantly beset by a confused stampede of emotions—jealousy, obsession, passion—each reigned briefly and then absconded. He struggled to shake off his internal chaos. Finally, he leaned forward and kissed Kelsey on the cheek.

"Congratulations."

"Is that all? Are we strangers?"

He thought, *What can I say to someone I loved and lost?*

But what escaped his lips was, "It's been a long time."

"Yes, it has. In any case, I'm glad to see you once more. Random images of you keep popping into my head," she said in barely a whisper.

Gallant hesitated, searching for the right words: "I'm sorry if I've intruded." He paused again. "I wish you a long and wonderful life."

Kelsey gave him a weak smile and said softly, "And I, you."

He thought he saw something in her eyes . . . sorrow . . . pity . . . regret? He couldn't be sure.

As he took a step to leave, he heard her whisper, "Goodbye, Henry."

The finality of those words stung his heart.

Outside the church, a bright and sunny day greeted the crowd, offering a rare tranquility for so late in the season. The verdant plants and trees added to the abiding peace and grace of the people as they leisurely formed a grand procession. Gallant watched as they began leaving for the banquet at the Hilton Hotel. It was a stellar turnout—celebrities, statesmen, and military men of all ranks and positions. No doubt that, as president of NNR, Gerome Neumann's status and money had attracted much attention to the young officer and his bride.

From the variety of the crowd's comportment—good-natured laughter, congratulatory handshakes, affectionate hugging—they could have been any group of family and friends gathering for a joyous event, yet Gallant could detect a subtle distinction, suggesting they were concealing a segregated trait. Noting the separation of wedding participants into one group that was invited to the reception and another that wasn't, Gallant assessed the invitees as the elite members of society—the so-called genetically superior. They included popular politicians, industrial giants, powerful lawyers, and social mavens, all supplicants of Gerome Neumann. Such was Gallant's intuition, harvested from his relations with his former shipmate, Anton Neumann.

A limousine pulled up near Gallant. The senior member of the family, Gerome Neumann, paraded down the steps toward the car. When he noticed Gallant, he scowled and stopped near him.

"Good day, sir," said Gallant.

"A good day, indeed," said Gerome Neumann as if to emphasize his personal triumph. "I am delighted with this match. Did you know my son was also promoted to command the *Achilles*? It's right that someone like him should enjoy success in all his endeavors. Don't you agree?" he asked in his dominating and demanding way.

"You mean someone with the right genetic qualifications?" asked Gallant, defiantly challenging the powerbroker.

"Yes. Someone with the physical improvements garnered through genetics that ensure he possesses the best hereditary traits."

"As opposed to a Natural like me," said Gallant, coaxing the senior Neumann to expose his personal convictions.

Gerome flashed a malevolent grin at the provocation: "Genetic engineering removes all the imperfections, thereby leaving—well—perfection! My son is blessed with all the gifts of an emerging superhuman race."

Gallant pushed aside his unruly hair as Gerome continued: "Finally, the right kind of men will go to the stars."

Gallant dared to look straight into Gerome's eyes and said, "Do you exclude someone like me—a less-than-perfect man—from the 'right' kind?"

Gerome's frown returned as he replied, "I've seen your genetic profile. You're a freak—a rare, random mutation. If you had taken my offer several years ago, things could have been different. You could have been useful. Now your erratic behavior has nullified any advantages. I've spoken to many others about you. Your genetic make-up leaves you as one of the underclass; merely a curiosity."

Gallant registered the insult. How far he had come in the last few years, and yet he was still light years away from being accepted. "I can only do my best."

"And what's that like?" asked Gerome.

"A work in progress."

"I don't recognize you as someone I want my son associated with. I want you to make every effort to steer clear of him." Gerome raised his voice for emphasis as he added, "And I will do what I can to help make that happen."

"Is the only way for your son to succeed—is for me to fail?"

"Ha," he scoffed. "You will fail regardless."

Gerome Neumann's words cut him, but Gallant regained his composure. "I will succeed—if only to prove you wrong."

"It's only fair to warn you that you're being watched." Gerome Neumann glared. "Do we understand each other?"

"Yes. I think we understand each other all too well."

Gerome shrugged before striking a pose for the crowd that had gathered around them. Raising his arms he said, "Thank you all for wishing my son well on his wedding day. Now, if you'll excuse me, I'm off to the reception."

Gallant watched him climb into his limousine as more than a door was slammed in his face.

6

ADMIRAL

The potent winter storms of Mars had not yet arrived, allowing the terraformed planet to enjoy a few more days of temperate weather and clear skies as Gallant strolled the cobblestone streets of New Annapolis, home of Fleet Command. Entering Fleet headquarters, Gallant was passed through security and turned over to Admiral Collingsworth's aide.

"Excuse me, Mr. Gallant?" asked the flag lieutenant.

"Yes."

"Follow me to the Admiral's suite."

Within a few minutes, Gallant was standing at attention in the vestibule of the admiral's office. The room was sparsely furnished, but it did display several historic artifacts that drew Gallant's attention. The walls were decorated with paintings of historic figures at moments of cataclysmic conflict.

Ever since he had read his orders placing him in command of the *Warrior*, Gallant had anticipated an interview with the admiral. Nevertheless, he felt ill-prepared, and he wondered if his uniform might not be pressed sharp enough, or his shoes might not be polished shiny enough, or his demeanor might not be proper enough to meet with the admiral's satisfaction.

A moment later the flag lieutenant's comm pin beeped and he said, "The admiral will see you now," and he pointed toward the door of the adjacent room.

Gallant strode purposefully through the archway and found the admiral seated at his desk. He marched into the center of the room, looked straight ahead, and saluted. "Lieutenant Gallant reporting as ordered, sir."

"Well?" said Collingsworth, as if expecting a more forthcoming salutation. He had a reputation as a fearless commander, a direct result of his personal combat experience. Never a man to be trifled with, his wrath had been felt by more than one dilettante—or fool.

Uncertain of the admiral's mood, Gallant couldn't think of how to respond to the abrupt question.

After a prolonged moment, Collingsworth finally intervened, releasing Gallant from twisting in the wind.

"Come closer. Come closer," he said pleasantly, sitting back in his well-cushioned chair. The wizened old man was immaculately dressed in a tailored uniform that enhanced his stature.

Gallant took three paces and stopped in front of the admiral's desk. He remained at attention.

"At ease," said the admiral. "It's been several years since I've seen you, Mr. Gallant."

Gallant relaxed his stance.

Collingsworth continued: "You've always been a source of wonderment for me, young man. You're aware, of course, that I've read the reports of your Tau Ceti exploits. Fascinating reading! Absolutely riveting! I couldn't put it down. Well done, by the way, though you wouldn't hear that through official channels, you understand."

"Yes, sir. I assume that mission played a role in getting my new command."

"Yes, you've proven to be an aggressive warrior—worthy of the *Warrior*," Collingsworth chuckled, pleased with his attempt at humor.

"I've merely done my duty, sir."

"Yes. Yes. I know. It's your duty to shoot the enemy," said the senior officer. "Of course, your unique talents have played an important role in our defense over the years. And your latest exploits highlighted your considerable ability to deal with artificial intelligence. Your talents will be especially needed for what I have in mind for you and the *Warrior*."

"Yes, sir."

The admiral's demeanor changed abruptly. His face became serious, and any hint of humor departed. "Your record on Tau Ceti has, unfortunately, been hidden behind a veil of secrecy, and most of the credit for the success of that mission has gone to Anton Neumann. While he was promoted, you retained the rank of lieutenant and were named as commander pro tem of the *Warrior*. That's the best I could do for you, given the high command's attitude."

"I am not aware of any professional failure on my part that would prevent my advancement," said Gallant warily.

"I'll come to the point: You should know that appointing you to command the first FTL stealth ship was my decision and my decision alone. There was a great deal of opposition to you, as I assume you can understand. You're a Natural—a talented one—but nevertheless, your lack of genetic engineering makes you suspect in the eyes of many in the service. They feel you will come up short at a critical moment."

Gallant shifted uneasily on his feet, frustrated by what was an unfair assessment of his abilities.

"They don't believe in you as I do, but the best way to give pause to their slander is to perform so that no one will believe the slurs," said the admiral with a furrowed brow. "Regardless, I'm assigning you this mission because I know you are the only person who can perform it. It is seriously dangerous, so I am allowing you wide discretion. That can be a two-edged sword. You must choose options that help you succeed; likewise, you will come to rely most upon those shipmates who can help you survive. And yet, in the end, you will put your closest comrades into the greatest danger for the sake of the mission."

The admiral seemed to shiver at his own words, as if he remembered only too well those he had likewise condemned.

"Gallant, part of being a leader is making tough choices—choices that sometimes decide the fate of others. A leader lives with those decisions by using the rationale that what he does is for the greater good, that many more lives will be spared because of the sacrifice of the few."

Gallant gave a slight nod.

"Choose wisely; you'll have to live with the outcome, whatever happens."

"Aye aye, sir."

The admiral stood and turned away from Gallant. "Time! I need time, Gallant. We have three technology breakthroughs that can change this war in our favor—a Faster-Than-Light drive, a powerful FASER cannon, and a stealth cloaking device. You already tested the FTL capability on the *Intrepid*. You also observed the FASER cannon when it was first fired from Ganymede. It can now be deployed on ships and has several times the firepower of a nuclear warhead on a small target area. Finally, I'm giving you our first stealth ship, the *Warrior*. We need time to put these technologies into full production. And you're going to buy me that time."

"Yes, sir," said Gallant, wondering how he was going to accomplish that.

"You may be wondering why SIA spent so much time with you interfacing with the Titan prisoners and their AI device."

"Yes, sir."

"I need someone to gather real-time intelligence of the enemy's intentions, someone who can understand their communications well enough to steal their most vital secrets. That someone is you. You're going to use what you have learned about their communications to conduct espionage and sabotage operations."

Gallant listened thoughtfully.

"You must be aware that this war is not going well. The fall of Jupiter Station has placed us in a precarious position. The Titan fleet is now closing its ring ever tighter toward Mars. The military losses in the last battle were huge. We threw everything we had into saving those colonists. The Titans slaughtered them anyway. If we fail, the people of Mars and Earth can expect no less. I have great hopes for your mission, Gallant—great hopes."

"I understand, sir."

"We've been driven from the Jupiter frontier; our colonies and mining operation in the asteroids have been devastated. NNR is our main shipping operator, and it took devastating losses, though the losses were highly insured and resulted in a nice government bonus for them. But the crews and other people were not so well compensated. In addition, the fleet collected no bonuses for fighting. We fight because we must."

"Yes, sir."

"We don't know the enemy's intentions. We can only react to their movements once they are observed. What we need is intelligence about what they're planning before they execute those plans. Give me that intelligence and I can fight more effectively."

"Yes, sir."

"You can achieve that with the spy equipment of the *Warrior*," said Collingsworth, returning to his chair. "My orders are for you to infiltrate the Titan bases around Jupiter and Saturn and bug their communications. Your ability to understand their autistic savant communications will aid you in gathering real-time intelligence so you can warn us of any impending attack. You will provide us with where and when they will strike so we can meet them on our terms. With that knowledge, we may survive long enough to produce the ships necessary to win this war. But that will rest, in large part, on your success."

Gallant was conscious of the admiral's eyes fixed on him, appraising his reaction.

"I will do my best, sir."

"The *Warrior* will be under my overall command, and I have written the orders for your mission. It will involve a great deal of independence on your part, and a great deal of responsibility as well. But I've found you up to the task before; I don't think you'll fail me now."

"I won't, sir."

"How long do you need to get the *Warrior* ready for departure?"

"Six days, sir. Less if I can get assistance expediting final deployment requirements."

Collingsworth glared at him: "She's completed shakedown?"

There was a shift in the atmosphere. Gallant could sense it. It was then he recognized there was some concern about his performance that needed to be accounted for.

Perhaps some latent concern about his being a Natural remained after all.

"Yes, sir."

"What is the state of upgrades for your ship?" asked the admiral.

"She is in the shipyard now completing upgrade calibration tests and final repairs. I can get the final supplies and personnel on board, make any necessary adjustments, and be prepared to leave in six days."

"Now let's discuss what you need from me."

"Of course, sir," said Gallant.

"What logistic requirements remain?"

"Specialized SIA equipment, listening recorder devices, and spare stealth components, sir."

Just hours before Gallant had been thinking of his personal relationships; now he was concentrating on military details in response to the admiral's demands.

"Send my aide a list of special assistance and supplies you need. He will look it over and see that your requests are expedited."

"Aye aye, sir."

Collingsworth instantly showed impatience and appeared flushed. "Recognize the spy business is not a game. It's not even a military operation. It is much more dangerous and subtle. Slight errors in judgment can mean more than just your life; they can mean the lives of many, many others."

"I understand, sir."

"Ultimately, war is a test of wills," said Collingsworth. "The one willing to do whatever it takes—to fight longer and harder—will prevail. Do you understand?"

"Yes, sir."

Filled with raw emotions, once more Collingsworth turned to Gallant and said, "Young man, buy me time!"

Gallant blushed and said, "I will, sir."

A pregnant moment passed.

Finally, Collingsworth's face relaxed and he said, "We will meet again under better circumstances, I'm sure." Extending his hand, the admiral concluded, "Good luck and good hunting, young man."

"Thank you, sir," said Gallant . . . *I'm going to need it.*

7

SHIPYARD

Orbiting 200 kilometers above Mars, the shipyard was an immense facility with an enclosed, two-kilometer central corridor at its center. Twenty-four docks extended from the central corridor and spiraled outward. Each dock could support a ship as large as a battle cruiser. Numerous minor ports also extruded from the core. Each ship rested in its dock where it could be refueled, repaired, or overhauled. There were several hundred meters of separation between the ships around which cranes and lifts could access various sections of individual ships. The shipyard was a city unto itself with a population of over 30,000 workers and residents. Since it had been constructed several decades earlier, it also provided support for the settlements on Phobos and Deimos. It serviced both military and commercial vessels, including merchants and ore ships primarily owned by NNR Shipping and Mining.

Following its shakedown cruise, the *Warrior* resided in docking bay number five while it underwent repairs from fire damage. Upgrades for specialized equipment designed for the ship's new mission were being handled by a combination of the ship's crew and shipyard experts.

All the berths were swarming with activity. Damaged ships that had been engaged in battle were being hauled into the remaining empty docks. Workers and military personnel bustled about their berths.

A sense of relief passed over Gallant when he found his ship under repair. He stood in the enclosed corridor surveying the *Warrior's* docking pier while workers continued their construction efforts.

Men in uniform and civilian shipyard workers were completing demanding tasks with wartime urgency. They loaded a wide variety of commodities including food, personal supplies, ammunition, fuel, and hydraulic oil. Crewmen were busily going over an inventory list and deciding where the equipment was to be stored. Along the passageway workers shepherded electronic equipment and complained that they had to get this done or their supervisor would complain. Gallant twisted around to see a many-storied crane hoisting out gigantic scaffolding for them to work from. There was an acetone smell nearby from recently completed welding.

Large, luminous lights bathed the outside of the ship as a small fleet of barges moved along its exterior to conduct repairs on the hull. Men in space suits crawled around the exposed surfaces of the ship. An almost continuous movement of the hoisting cranes brought machinery and equipment to the workers. Even so, the progress in shipyards is always slower than any captain would like.

Gallant tried to visualize the *Warrior* complete and ready for action. He touched the virtual green display of a nearby console and activated the inventory list of remaining tasks. He then visited the ship's dock supervisor.

Each berth had a dock supervisor who was responsible for the correct and timely completion of each ship's work order. There was one shipyard supervisor who directed all the other supervisors, and he was known simply as the "inspector." He met with the dock supervisors each morning in a small control shack at the edge of the central corridor and set their priorities. Over coffee and sandwiches they discussed current construction decisions about schedule, personnel, and supplies for all the ships currently being serviced. The supervisors were all able engineers with good business sense, but they were always looking over their shoulders for politically correct directives.

When Gallant first ran into this cabal of construction managers, he was slightly intimidated by their seniority, but as he became familiar with the station's operations, he devoted more of his time with them to ensuring that his ship was given the priority it needed.

As he walked into the supervisor's shack adjacent to the *Warrior's* berth, he was greeted with a loud growl.

"What do you want?" barked a small man with a hawk-like nose and slicked-down hair. He was sitting on an uncomfortable looking chair at the single desk in the small office.

Finally looking up from his work, he stood when he recognized Gallant. "Sorry, sir. I didn't know you were here. Is there something I can help you with?"

"Yes. The *Warrior* is behind schedule. I need the work expedited."

"Yes, sir. The schedule is right here," said the supervisor handing it to him.

"I am aware of the schedule. The problem is we're not on schedule. What are you doing about that?"

"We're making good progress, and I can see daylight. You should realize this work takes time. There's a war on, you know," he chuckled, pleased with himself. "I have to yield to other shipyard priorities set by the inspector, you know," he said, shrugging as if he had dealt with many complaining captains before and was not impressed by a mere lieutenant.

Gallant stood quietly for a moment. He could hear a far-off hiss of fresh air exiting ventilation ducts, the drone of air conditioners struggling against the heat, and the many other machines adding to the noise pollution.

The supervisor sensed his mood and said, "Don't worry, sir. I'll have everything on track before you know it. I was here a year ago when the NNR Company first laid down this ship's keel." He said it with some sense of pride, but Gallant surmised it was a token of intimidation to show his seniority and the authority of NNR.

The thought came to Gallant that everyone and everything were conspiring to delay the *Warrior's* departure. If he had any sense, he would go running to the admiral's aide and beg for additional assistance, but the admiral might see that as a lack of ability on his part.

Instead, Gallant decided to redouble his efforts and reevaluate key component upgrades—supervising their installation himself. He was aware that several of his officers and the supervisor would not be pleased with his direct involvement. They would interpret it as a slight, but he couldn't help that. The jobs needed to get done, and he could not trust to happenstance that they would be completed on time.

He left the shack and went to work. Tests for all kinds of equipment—electronic, mechanical, and hydraulic—were scheduled. Hour by hour new problems and delays occurred as fast as existing jobs were being completed.

After three arduous days, despite some remaining concerns, there was progress. Before he began the final walk-through inspection of the *Warrior* with his officers, Gallant gave the crew a short liberty. Four hours wasn't much for a crew about to deploy for months on a hazardous mission, but it was all Gallant could afford.

There was a mad rush to shower and change into a liberty uniform. The crew could not have been quicker to leave the ship if she were on fire from stem to stern. Four hours was barely enough time to reach a New Annapolis tavern and return. But their thirst could be quenched and they could enjoy one last good meal.

Not a single man returned late, and only one never left.

"Chief Howard, why aren't you on liberty?" Gallant asked.

"I've been on liberty before, sir. Besides, there's no way you're going to inspect my ship without me."

Chief Howard and Gallant marched through the ship, stopping in every compartment while the responsible officer presented it for their inspection. Chief Howard kept a watchful eye and maintained a complete log of all remaining deficiencies.

The walk-through began in the operations compartment where Roberts reported some problem areas, though none were critical to meeting deployment requirements.

In engineering, Walker reported a serious problem with the dark matter engine that could only be addressed using a gigantic crane.

In CIC, Clay reported a critical problem with the stealth technology that required calibration using shipyard equipment. He also complained about calibration of the Wasp's stealth system. He made it clear he expected trouble with the new technology.

"Thank you, gentlemen," Gallant said. "I will be leaving to see the shipyard inspector shortly. Please provide detailed specifications to Chief Howard about the identified deficiencies."

As the officers returned to their duties, Gallant said, "Mr.Clay, will you join me in my cabin?"

"Aye aye, sir."

Clay followed Gallant to the door of the captain's cabin. Clean-shaven with freshly trimmed hair, Clay tended to display a lack of patience and often exposed his aggressive nature. Gallant realized he was going to have a difficult time dealing with his weapons officer.

"At ease. Have a seat," Gallant said. "From your weapons report, it's going to take a great deal of resources and manpower over a period of several days before the stealth system will be fully operational."

"Yes, sir."

"Please give me your frank assessment of the operational readiness of the ship."

"All weapons systems are ready with the exception of the stealth technology," Clay said. "I am still finding calibration flaws, and there remains an issue with the battery charging that causes leakage which reduces the charge lifetime."

Gallant didn't let his focus wander: "You'll be responsible for getting these systems operational. I will arrange for assistance from the shipyard, but you will be held strictly accountable."

"I need to do a recalibration of the system using the shipyard equipment."

Gallant bit his tongue and said, "If we get a recalibration, do you think it will hold up on deployment?"

"I can't say for sure, sir, but without a recalibration, there is no chance at all."

"Alright. Once we depart, I want a weekly report. You're going to spend a great deal of time in this cabin briefing me."

"Aye aye, sir."

"I want you to make arrangements to keep the force shield up. See if we can get equipment and men to support our efforts."

"Yes, sir."

"We have only one Wasp with stealth technology, so we'll have to test it thoroughly."

"I'll get Chief Howard started on it."

"Good. I expect you to supervise all operations. I want maximum cooperation."

"Aye aye, sir."

As a classmate of Anton Neumann, Clay didn't have to explicitly state his reasons for being dissatisfied with his commanding officer, but Gallant recognized the look on his face—it was all too familiar—a look born of doubt over his genetic background.

8

DELICATE TOUCH

Gallant swallowed his queasiness as the blustery gale wind whipped the space elevator's cable about—causing an erratic acceleration which rocked the glass vehicle like ocean swells rolling against a ship's hull. He hoped the braking system was still sound as they approached the ground platform at seven g's.

When at last he escaped the miniature craft, he found his legs a little wobbly. It was late morning when he reached SIA headquarters and asked to see LCDR McCall.

"Here's a copy of my orders, Commander," he said to the SIA agent when he was ushered into her office. He reached over her desk to hand her the tablet, but she didn't take it immediately.

Her wispy blond hair was cut in a smart style and her well-tailored uniform drew attention to her curvaceous figure. She stared at him with her dark blue eyes exuding a mischievous boldness as if she expected him to comment in a particular way. After a moment she looked disappointed as she reached out and took his tablet.

"Well, Lieutenant, I'll need some additional information."

He nodded.

"You've had several personal relationships over the years. Are you involved with someone special now?"

"I beg your pardon," he responded lamely. Surely, she had been through his file and was well-briefed on him.

She got up and went to the coffee station across the room and returned a minute later with two cups.

As he sipped the brew, she studied his orders, sifting through the documents. She handed him back the tablet with several forms to fill out and sign. As he did so, he was amazed at how often this process involved her touching his arm, or hand. It was surprising how small the office now seemed.

Was that deliberate? What's she playing at?

Gallant was flattered by the close personal attention of a beautiful woman, but even as the blood course through his veins, he was uncertain about what kind of situation he might be getting into.

She started to asked, "Would you like to . . ."

They were startled as a captain burst into the room.

Gallant stood and came to attention.

The captain gave McCall a pointed look and handed something to her. As he left he said, "Carry on."

McCall's attitude was all business now and she said, "These are some tests for you to take. It's part of our ENIGMA research, so we can evaluate your progress in translating the Titan messages."

Taking the tablet, Gallant started the first test and breezed right through it.

He paused from the testing process and commented, "Their approach to numbers is fascinating once you examine how they manipulate them."

McCall asked, "What do you mean?"

"Think of the number one as if it were a smooth pebble on the beach. Now think of the number five as five individual pebbles on the beach in the shape of an L; with three pebbles forming the vertical part of the letter and two pebbles as the horizontal base of the letter."

He drew on the tablet:

5
5
555

"OK," she nodded.

"Now; picture of the number seven as an L-shaped configuration of pebbles with four in a vertical column and three pebbles forming the horizontal base."

Again he drew,

7
7
7
7777

In fact, all odd numbers can be represented as L-shaped groups of pebbles."

"What does that accomplish?"

"If we add consecutive odd numbers together, we get 1 + 3 = 4, 1 + 3 + 5 = 9, and 1 + 3 + 5 + 7 = 16, and so on. Can you see that combining odd numbers this way produces squares, 4, 9, and 16? The insight you can find is that when you stack images of L-shaped objects together (1 + 3 + 5 + 7) you build square shaped objects (16). Try it for yourself, draw them out."

She drew the representation of 16 pebbles,

7531
7533
7555
7777

"Huh. So you think that's how the Titans perform their mathematical thinking—by combining natural shapes into geometric objects to find visual solutions."

Gallant said, "Yes. It's rather a different exercise in understanding and manipulating numbers. If we add to that the other sensory perceptions they combine with their communications it gets rather complicated. Sometimes, I find that their language is like listening to the music. The sensory evolutions are magnificent, filled with emotions and thrills, even if you don't understand the words."

"I've a feeling you're going to be rather good at translating their messages," she said.

"I hope so."

"Oh, you have a unique talent, but don't overestimate your abilities. Do you think you're going to win this war all by yourself?" she asked.

Gallant said, "No, but I believe I have a role to play."

"Things don't always end well for those who are different and can't fit in. So—Natural talent—or not, you need to get better at translating."

He blushed,

Was that a genetic slur?

Later, on the seventh subfloor, Gallant continued his communication training with the prisoners under McCall's watching eye. While savant syndrome was exceedingly rare in humans, it could produce astonishing islands of ability or brilliance. As he studied the alien's savant skills, he saw them exhibit prodigious memory and superior mathematical skills, as well as, extraordinary sensory sensitivity.

"I think I'll nickname this prisoner, 'Raymond,'" said Gallant.

"Raymond? Why would you do that?" asked McCall.

"It's a reference to an old movie about an autistic savant who displayed remarkable intellectual talent, but was unable to function productively, or independently, due to profound social deficits," said Gallant. "I think it suits him."

She nodded and then said, "We're built from very small particles, but we live in a very large universe. We only see visible light which is a trillionth of the electromagnetic waves traveling across the universe because we aren't equipped with the right sensory receptions to find them all. However, some animals, such as, the echo locating bat can use other waves to understand the world around it. Perhaps the Titans have extrasensory receptors too."

"Possibly," said Gallant. "Our brains interpret signals from our senses and we're forced to accept the reality it shows us, but reality could be very different to the Titans."

She said, "Gallant, just as the blind learn to read braille with his fingers, you need to find a way to read the Titan's sensory output and understand its meaning."

Gallant nodded, but wondering,

What's her agenda?

9

RAID

The first winter storm blew through New Annapolis with a ferocity that dwarfed much humbler Earth hurricanes, deluging streets and buildings with such intensity that it washed away all traces of color, stripping the trees of their leafy green foliage, packing inky-black mud over the red-brown cobblestones of the streets, strewing branches and debris over the well-manicured lawns of stately homes, and blowing away the decorative signage of the craft and trade shops. And it was this forfeiture of color, above all else, that transformed the quiet, graceful, rustic town's warmth and identity into a dull gray-black facsimile of its former self.

The *Warrior* remained in the shipyard undergoing repairs from its shakedown cruise and upgrading equipment to meet the requirements for its new mission. Meanwhile Gallant consoled himself that the shipyard was high above the planet and safe from the vicious weather as he made his way into the underground bowels of SIA headquarters. A dozen of his crew members were also at the underground facilities going through intensive training in communications, sabotage, and stealth operations.

After completing his daily study program, Gallant was prepared to return to his ship, but due to the weather, the space elevator was inoperable and he was stranded planetside. So he decided to visit a friend, or two. He left SIA headquarters and planting one foot in front of another, it occurred to him,

It's not till the first gale of winter that you find out what will carry away.

Anyone left outside in the furious tempest felt the oppressive force of the wind trying to swoosh them away. A timid man would not go out under these conditions, which wouldn't have been such an awful thing if there were no particular place for him to go, or if there were no particular person for him to see, but the weather didn't deter Gallant.

Chilled through and through despite his so-called "weatherproof" clothing, he made his way toward the local refugee camp where he planned to inquire about missing friends. He continued to brave the misery of the storm until he heard the sirens shriek.

EEEEEEERRRR!!!

He cursed,
Oh, no. It's started already.

He had been monitoring the news reports for several days, as had all inhabitants of the inner planets, anxious for any update of the approaching crisis. Over one hundred Titan destroyers and cruisers in twenty separate raiding parties were approaching Mars, Earth, and Venus. Intercepting them meant dividing the UP fleet and weakening the defense against a follow-up massive strike toward a specific planet of the Titans' choosing. The alien ships could cruise ten percent faster than their UP counterparts, which complicated the interception calculus. Fleet Command evaluated its optimal strategy for intercepting the raiders to preclude them from launching nuclear missiles at the occupied worlds. UP ships flew for several days to intercept the enemy.

Panic lay just beneath the surface and raw nerves grew tighter with each passing day as they waited for events to unfold.

Now, for the first time since the start of the war, Mars experienced the sirens of an impending attack. People left their homes and defied the storm to run to the bomb shelters distributed throughout the city.

Chaos reigned.

It was as if Gallant had stepped into another world. The crowds of New Annapolis pressed against the railing at the entrances to a local shelter—safety lay on the other side. A megaphone from a security guard called, "Remain calm! There's room for everyone!"

Windows rattled and doors shook as scores of antimissile missiles were launched.

"What's the latest news?" Gallant asked, as strangers rushed by. No one stopped to answer, but one man called back over his shoulder, "Take shelter!"

"A raid? Is the raid targeting here?" demanded Gallant. As the man kept running, he wondered,

Where's the fleet?

The sirens let out a continual maddening scream, indicating that an assault was imminent. The defense forces prepared to meet the approaching ships. The planet's space fighters were sent to intercept the incoming missiles, but they were few, and the missiles were many. Distant surface missile silos launched a series of antimissile missiles filling the skies with swooshing sounds. The antimissiles swooshed up into the sky to intercept the enemy and destroy them before their warheads could explode. Even from the street Gallant could see the space station high above firing missiles to protect the city, but some Titans seemed to have broken through the defensive ring.

There came a sonic boom.

Then another.

Gallant heard the whistling screams of antimissiles leaving the ground batteries and climbing to strike down the incoming threats. Bursts of detonations arose high in the air from one end of the horizon to the other. The sky was alive with the deadly dance of combat as broken warheads and destroyed fighters fell to earth. Far off rumblings of explosions from destroyed weapons crashing to the ground.

Gallant tried to see who was winning,

Deliverance?

There was still time for him to seek shelter like everyone else, but he wasn't so inclined. He remained at the entrance to the shelter without entering, foregoing his safety for an opportunity to witness the attack. But remaining above ground left him to nearly suffocate from the wind, debris, and dust swirling past him.

Unfortunately, one of the enemy missiles managed to break through the defenses. Its nuclear warhead exploded about 200 kilometers north of New Annapolis in what was, thankfully, a fallow region of the continent. Nevertheless, the nuclear explosion produced a devastating red fireball plume. The edge of the shock wave followed soon after. Broken branches twirled and fluttered from the heavens; they were all that remained of the forest a hundred kilometers away.

As the latecomers streamed into the shelters, Gallant could count himself among the procrastinators, disbelievers, and fools—all of whom had waited too long—as he finally ducked into the protection of the shelter just in time to avoid the effects of the blast as it passed through the town. Somehow, the damage did not seem too severe. He was more concerned about his ship. How would it fare if it were hit by a missile? Again he cursed his bad luck of being stranded planet-side at such a critical time.

Finally, the defense force succeeded in destroying the remaining Titan threat.

Gallant didn't know exactly how long it was until the all clear was finally given, but he gave a sigh of relief when it was. The hurricane had not yet blown itself out, and the gray skies kept their bluster. It seemed unreal—grotesquely unreal. The skies were colors he had never seen before, and they were filled with smoke that hung over the area suffocating everything with malodorous fumes from explosions and exhaust. Attempts to restore order were underway, but the "all clear" left the New Annapolis population disoriented and confused. The sharp crackling of ships flashing overhead was from small craft of all kinds shuttling men and supplies to emergency sites. The roads were choked with emergency vehicles and military cars of all kinds. People, concerned about their loved ones, would have to wait, at least for now.

Gallant didn't know if the space station was still intact, or if his ship and crew were hurt. He had to find out, but he was slow to realize that was not yet possible. All communications were down; most electronic systems had been knocked out by the electromagnetic pulse from the nuclear blast.

With few other options to occupy his time until the space elevator was restored, Gallant decided to take the underground monorail to the refugee camp to investigate whether someone he knew had been hurt or if there was anything he could do to help.

When he reached the camp he found the exiles had been reluctant to leave their homes when the siren had sounded. They should have gone to the shelters, but they remembered the false hope the shelters on Ganymede had provided to the souls still buried inside of them. Many had simply halted and waited until the all clear was sounded as if they didn't understand their dilemma.

10

REFUGEE CAMP

The rag-tag refugee camp on the outskirts of New Annapolis also suffered from a lack of color, only it had been without pigmentation long before the storm and the traumatic Titan raid had hit. Its gray, prefabricated buildings constructed from frail material and sundry supplies were all that shielded the desperate outcasts who sought shelter and solace. The camp never enjoyed the luxury of green trees, red-brown cobblestones, stately homes, or decorative shops. It was, and remained, a dark, monochromatic community—a grim illustration of its own dismal future.

The refugees represented a lost society from a stark community. They had been hearty pioneers colonizing satellites and chunks of rock millions of kilometers from Earth. But now, war had achieved a greater reality for these individual survivors—it had killed their families and destroyed their homes. It had forced them millions of kilometers from their heritage. Built as a temporary settlement, the camp held over 100,000 individuals. Run by a government agency with the assistance of charity and relief organizations, it was set up in an impromptu fashion designed to meet only the most basic human needs for a short time. Due to crowding and a lack of infrastructure, some sections of the refugee camp were unhygienic, leading to a high incidence of infectious diseases. The camp administrators worked night and day to prevent a humanitarian crisis.

Grateful the underground monorail was still running, Gallant traveled to the refugee camp to search for his friends. Not knowing their fate was worse than hearing bad news.

The aliens had traveled in sublight generation ships from Gleise-581 and had colonized the outer planets of the Solar System. Gallant and some of his friends had fought the aliens several years earlier. He hadn't heard from many of them since.

Gallant found an information depot, but the computer data offered little help—too much of the available data was vague and uncorrelated. However, after asking a camp worker, he was able to trace one individual. That person was staying on the edge of the camp in a small room of an apartment building. Following the side streets through the camp, Gallant soon found the man he was looking for.

"Hello, Henry," said Jacob Bernstein when he answered the knock on his door.

"It's been quite a while, Jake. How are you?" Gallant looked at the thin haggard old man, seeing the years of suffering in his eyes.

"Well enough," said Jake as the wind reeled past the thin windows. "It's just this miserable cold."

"I never thought I would see you on Mars," said Gallant, "but I'm glad you were one of the survivors."

"It's the war," said the old man shaking his head. "It goes on and on; too much death and destruction."

"Can you get any news updates about the raid yet?" asked Gallant eager to find if there was an update.

"Come here," Jake said as he pulled Gallant toward a view screen. They settled into seats next to a messy table filled with stacks of plates and miscellaneous items. After a few minutes of futile scanning of channels, Jake said, "There's nothing but emergency communications and orders to remain in place and keep calm. No news about casualties or the status of the fleet."

"Tell me what happened at Jupiter," Gallant said.

"It was a blessing you weren't there," Jake said. He sighed before adding: "It was a hell of a fight, a real heroic effort. Even in defeat, our people were magnificent. The sacrifice was huge. You have to have faith in what we're fighting for or it would never be worth that kind of loss. After the Titans defeated our fleet, they used nuclear bombs on the colonies. We fled. Several squadrons of UP cruisers and destroyers tried to cover the evacuation."

Gallant listened as Jake provided details.

"On the first day of the evacuation, only several thousand were able to shuttle to transports. On the second day the marine rearguard held an insignificant sliver of a volcanic crater around the capital city of Kendra. Thanks to their efforts and supported by a few remaining destroyers and numerous small craft, a full day of the evacuation was successful. On the third day, people escaped aboard small craft running from the moons to larger ships. A wide variety of small vessels from all over the asteroids and nearby moons were pressed into service to aid in the evacuation. A flotilla of hundreds of merchant ships, mining ships, pleasure craft, and salvage vessels were brought into service. The withdrawal was chaotic using whatever could fly, all of them packed with refugees."

Jake's gaze fixed on Gallant's face, reading his reaction.

Jake continued: "The Titan armada engaged with the remnants of our fleet while splinter squadrons attacked the colonies. It was on the third day that the Titan destroyers focused on the marine pockets holding out at Ganymede. They held fast until the fourth day. The remaining battalion was massacred when the men ran out of ammunition for their heavy weapons,"

His voice broke as he spoke, "My son was one of them."

He concluded quietly, "Jupiter Station was destroyed the next day."

Gallant sat in silent company.

Pounding his fist into his hand, Jake said, "I'd like to give them a taste of their own medicine. I'd like to have the pleasure of driving them from their homes one day."

Gallant remained for a while before taking his leave. He shook hands with Jake and gave him a comm address so they could stay in contact. Then he checked on the space elevator.

A cold and bitter wind blustered down the street as he reached the elevator. He pulled his coat closer around him and jammed his hands into his pockets. He plowed forward, leaning into the wind, his nose running. He didn't allow himself to seek the warmth of a nearby building. He was determined to reach the entry port,

I need to get back to my ship.

11

OVERTIME

Gallant passed bustling workers completing jobs on a dozen ships as he made his way through the central corridor and into the main administration building on his way to the shipyard inspector's office. The office had glass walls that offered a panoramic view of the entire shipyard. The inspector was scrunched over his desk console reviewing ship status reports.

Gallant extended his hand and said, "Hello, inspector. I'm the commanding officer of the *Warrior*—dock five."

"Yes. I know who you are," he said with complete indifference. In a sweeping gesture, he brought his hands to his chest and said, "I know everything about what goes on in my shipyard."

Gallant pulled back his neglected hand and said, "I'm sure you do, but I have several concerns that..."

But the inspector interrupted: "You should address your issues to your dock supervisor. If there is anything important enough to warrant my involvement, he'll inform me." Then he returned his attention to his console.

Gallant tapped the inspector on the shoulder.

As the man turned, his face froze and he turned his nose up. He knew what was coming.

In a strident voice Gallant said, "You're responsible for completing repairs and upgrades as specified in your contract—on time and within specifications—or else the ship's commanding officer may refuse payment authorization. It would then become a matter for the admiralty and the NNR Shipping and Mining Company to resolve."

The inspector pruned his lips together. "Young man, there is simply no need to magnify a simple issue into gigantic proportions."

Gallant continued: "My officers and I have completed our ship walk-through inspection, and I'm gravely disappointed. The dock supervisor—and you—have signed off on many completed items that I've found deficient."

Gallant handed the inspector a tablet list of considerable length.

"Lieutenant, may I speak frankly?" The inspector was several decades Gallant's senior, and his distain showed.

"By all means; please do so," said Gallant drawing himself up to his maximum height, towering over the slight man.

"Let me tell you, we prioritized the essential repairs and upgrades that were authorized. I personally oversaw that the critical requirements were met to our highest standards. The trivial items you've identified as remaining are not worth bothering about. Your ship's engineering team can fix those on your deployment. I have other warships under repair with the highest priority; I can't take the time to make everything all nice and pretty for your fancy tastes."

Holding his temper, Gallant said, "This ship has a vital mission utilizing unique technology that must be fully operational and expertly calibrated from the moment we depart this station. The capabilities of this ship include extraordinary systems requiring a great deal of state-of-the-art electronic gear. It's essential that everything perform at peak efficiency, and tinkering with them while on deployment is not my idea of professional performance."

"I'm not sure I understand you. What kind of systems are we talking about?"

Gallant was fully aware that the *Warrior* might find herself in combat from the instant she left the dock. "I'm referring to the stealth cloaking device and the dark matter engine. This ship gives us a chance to do things no other ship can, but only if the systems are properly attuned. We have to rely on their robustness. We may be hundreds of millions of kilometers from Mars, and if those systems fail, we will have no one to call for help. The lives of my crew depend on those systems performing properly."

"I'm sorry. I don't mean to be pessimistic, but I don't know how to accomplish everything you require. In my opinion, there are always bugs in new systems that only operational experience can wash out," said the inspector as he rolled his eyes and spread his arms wide, as if asking for divine guidance.

They stood glaring at each other for several more moments.

Unable to take the silence, Gallant said, "You're a real character, but we view our roles very differently."

The supervisor frowned and shrugged. "My men and I have done everything possible to see that this ship will do just fine. Don't go making trouble. You need to sign off on these repairs and accept responsibility for the ship." The man wagged his finger at Gallant, "I've done my duty; now go do yours."

Gallant could restrain his anger no longer. "I fail to see your so-called duty coming into play here. I'm responsible to see that you do your job. I want you to recall your engineering crew and get to work completing the items on this list. Otherwise, I won't sign off."

The inspector looked away and snorted. He shook his head causing the hair to rise on the back of his neck. Then he stuck out his chin as if anticipating the worst, but with a cool grin he said, "If you think I'll do that, you're mistaken."

A sigh escaped Gallant's pressed lips as he fought to maintain his composure.

The grin on the inspector's face widened as if he believed he had gained the upper hand. "I made a request earlier today, but I haven't received the documentation, the equipment, or the support personnel that I would need to complete the work you wish."

"There'll be an investigation if this isn't done properly and on time," Gallant said carefully, knowing that any investigation would come too late to serve his purpose.

"You're straining my neck by making me look up at you. Shift around so I can get a better look," said the inspector.

Gallant didn't move. "This is ridiculous. Why can't you come out and state the obvious truth that you're behind schedule, and you have failed to meet certain specifications?"

The inspector pouted and said, "You're stuck, lieutenant. I've seen your departure date. You've got to get going. There's no time to do everything you want. Just sign off and be done with it."

"I see you're feeling quite proud of yourself, aren't you?"

"I'm only trying to do my job."

Gallant spread his hands and said, "Let me put my cards on the table: Things need a lot of adjustments, and my crew will be working around the clock to make them. One serious problem is the need to calibrate the stealth equipment. It requires specialized equipment and expertise that is only available at this shipyard." He leaned close to the little man and showed him a new list: "This is a reduced list identifying our most critical remaining requirements. They must be completed in twenty-four hours, or I'll be unable to perform my mission."

The revised list was one tenth the length of the original.

The inspector warmed to the compromise. He said, "Good. You're thinking more clearly at last, lieutenant. This list is possible. I might be able to get a crew working—on overtime—mind you," said the inspector as he rubbed his chin. "Are you willing to authorize overtime pay—with bonuses?"

Gallant sighed,

There it is. That's what he's been angling for all along.

He swallowed hard and said, "I'll authorize the NNR overtime pay and bonuses." He extended his hand and added, "I appreciate your cooperation, inspector."

The inspector pumped his hand. Gallant had no doubt that the inspector's personal bonus would be substantial—not to mention the reward NNR would bestow on him for closing this account to their advantage.

Twenty four hours later, the *Warrior* completed all critical repairs and upgrades.

12

ORDERS

Seated in his cabin aboard the *Warrior*, Gallant read—and then reread—his secret orders. Admiral Collingsworth had promised an ambitious mission, but the daring and scope of the proposal before him took his breath away. His mission was divided into two phases. The first phase was to disrupt the Titan war capacity by spying, intriguing, and sabotaging the Titan fleet and its bases around Jupiter and Saturn. The second phase would remain under sealed orders until the first phase was satisfactorily completed. While sealed orders were normal enough, they placed him in the awkward situation of suppressing his natural curiosity. Reluctantly, he placed the package of sealed orders back in his safe and locked it.

Turning his attention to the phase one instructions and their associated parcels, he sorted the different documents and the special devices accompanying them. He undertook to study the contents. The items included electronic monitoring equipment, some of which he found unfamiliar, so he put them aside for the time being. There were also supplemental guidelines for various options he could undertake during the course of the mission; those, too, he put aside. His need to be thorough led him to read the main document through twice. Then he rose and began pacing in the confined cabin—five steps forward, five steps back—all that space allowed. Soon he sat back down, only to get up again and resume pacing. Overall, he was impressed with the generous leeway the admiral had allowed him. He was tempted to keep the main sections of his orders secret from his officers. But he recognized that wouldn't be fair.

Gallant summoned his officers to the wardroom. Roberts, Clay, Walker, Gabriel, and several others were crammed into the diminutive room. Only the duty officers were absent. As senior chief, Chief Howard was included.

"Gentlemen, I would like to share with you the gist of our mission statement and read you into this special operations program."

The complete silence spoke volumes about their anticipation. All eyes were glued on Gallant, except for Gabriel's, who sat with his mouth slightly agape and staring intently at the orders in his captain's hands.

"Over the next few months," Gallant said, "we will be conducting special operations in Titan territory, in particular Jupiter and Saturn; code name ULTRA. In preparation for these activities, we will conduct extensive stealth training on our journey to Jupiter."

Gallant didn't mention the far-reaching alien communications language studies he would have to undergo. He kept that to himself along with his apprehension that his translation skills would be stretched to their limits.

The quiet murmur was quickly overwhelmed by noisy chatter as the men reacted excitedly to the news.

After a minute of patience, Gallant silenced the gathering once more.

"We will be completely on our own with no support of any kind, so we must be frugal with everything we have and everything we do. That includes protecting each other and our crew. We are all we have. So do your best, knowing we serve a mighty purpose."

A hush hung over the room until Gabriel exclaimed, "Wow, I can't wait!"

Everyone looked at him, and then a boisterous laughter broke out.

Howard chuckled, "*Youth* is fleeting—*old* lasts a lot longer."

An hour later, there was a knock on Gallant's cabin door.

"Enter."

"Hello, Henry," said Lieutenant Commander McCall.

Standing as she entered the cabin, Gallant said, "Commander, I thought you completed your business with

CIC. We've just stationed the maneuvering watch. We depart within the hour. Is there something else I can do for you?"

The SIA agent sat down on his cot and handed him a tablet. Surprised, Gallant took the tablet and began reading the set of orders. When he was through he slowly sat down.

"This can't be right," he said, frowning.

"And why not?" asked the blonde with a coy expression.

"I've had no prior instructions regarding taking a passenger on our mission."

"Not a passenger—a special agent," she corrected in a pleasant but authoritative voice, "specifically tasked to analyze and evaluate the data you acquire."

Gallant stared at her, contemplating his new circumstances. Having an SIA agent make intelligence judgments on the military material they gathered—right at its source—made sense. It would increase Fleet Command's confidence in the intelligence the *Warrior* sent, but why choose McCall? Gallant recalled her fixation with his talents. Was there more to her assignment than the orders revealed?

Gallant tapped his comm pin: "Bridge, this is the captain; have the XO report to my cabin."

A moment later Roberts poked his head into the doorway and said, "You wanted to see me, skipper?"

"Come in, XO."

Roberts squeezed into the congested cabin.

"Mr. Roberts, this is Lieutenant Commander McCall. She has special expertise in Titan communications and will serve as SIA liaison to CIC during our mission."

"Err, yes, sir."

"Commander McCall, I'm pleased that we will have your skills available during this undertaking. I think you'll find our CIC techs are well prepared, but I am sure they will welcome your input. I look forward to consulting with you when we prepare our findings and recommendations for Fleet Command."

McCall smiled and said, "Captain, I will, of course, in no way interfere with your command decisions while aboard this ship, but with all due respect, I expect to have rather more say than merely providing input to CIC. You've read my orders. I am to adjudicate findings and conclusions drawn from any collected intelligence."

"Actually, that's not my interpretation of your orders. And aboard my ship, I insist upon having the final word in all matters—captain's privilege. I'm sure you understand."

McCall stood and scrutinized each man in turn. Gallant stood and stared back at her, his jaw set. He made the assessment that while she had no intention of being limited by his politely delineated boundaries, she was weighing how much she needed to push back at this precise moment.

"As you say, captain's privilege," and she bowed her head in apparent acquiescence.

"You can take up your duties immediately," Gallant said. "We'll arrange a data management meeting in CIC after we get underway. I would appreciate your written plan of action for dealing with critical intelligence as we acquire it."

McCall hesitated a moment under Gallant's sharp gaze before she said, "I'll have the report within a day."

She seemed to recognize that by agreeing to his first demand she was ceding him more authority than she wished to acknowledge. "Also, I would like to send a message to SIA before we leave, to clarify our understanding of my role aboard."

"I'm sorry, commander, but the ship is now under a communications blackout per our mission orders."

McCall's clenched teeth convinced Gallant that he had dealt adequately with what might have become a difficult situation. He began to plan his activities for the ship's departure.

"Mr. Roberts, I'm sorry to inconvenience you, but I am assigning your cabin to Commander McCall. You will have to double up with members of the wardroom. I'll leave the arrangements to you."

Gallant was distinctly pleased with himself for phrasing that demand as he did since every cubic meter aboard the sloop was already accounted for, several times over. How Roberts was going to find any spare room was difficult to imagine.

Roberts, already uncomfortable after witnessing the exchange between the senior officers, was now doubly so at finding he was to lose his stateroom as well.

"Aye aye, sir. Is there anything else, sir?"

"Yes. Please show Commander McCall to her cabin. Thank you; that will be all."

From the look McCall gave Gallant as she left—that wouldn't be all.

※

Gallant posted the less sensitive parts of the phase one orders in the crew's mess, and the *Warrior* set course toward the asteroid belt. Before long she was weaving past large rocks and blasting small ones.

The crew's drills improved their proficiency in deploying and recharging the stealth technologies. Several crew members, who had attended specialized school at SIA, were now able to pass their newly acquired knowledge on to their shipmates.

The mission was so highly dependent on communications that Gallant considered replacing Gabriel as communication officer. Roberts met with him to discuss this point and championed replacing Gabriel.

To his own surprise, Gallant said, "No. I won't replace him. We'll support him. He'll be fine," thereby putting the matter to rest.

13

CONVOY

Gallant's cabin was pitch-black with the exception of several flickering lights on the ship's status console above his head. He took note that all the lights were green—no red lights meant no emergencies. He took a deep breath and exhaled slowly while remaining curled up on his side, semi-conscious, listening to the routine noises around him—the incessant whistling from the ventilation, the repetitious groaning of the bulkheads, and the buzzes, beeps, and honks, emanating from control consoles on the bridge a dozen meters away.

A single sharp ping from the bridge caused him to sit up, alert. He stretched fretfully, pulling his thoughts together, and glanced at the chronometer. He prepared to get up, but the warmth of the bed tempted him to use the few moments of grace left to him to rest. Already dressed from having slept in his uniform, he touched the AI console for a quick report of the ship's operating parameters.

Everything looked nominal; nevertheless, he threw his legs over the side of the bed and waited for the report.

"Captain to the bridge!" blared from the overhead speaker.

He bolted out the door, into the passageway, and bolted the dozen steps to the bridge.

"Captain on the bridge," said the officer of the deck.

"Carry on," said Gallant, his eyes sweeping the control displays, looking for alerts.

The bridge crew continued their duties, but their intense faces told Gallant they were keyed up for action.

"Contacts?" he asked.

The OOD said, "We have three large contacts at the edge of radar range, sir."

"Show me."

Gallant slipped into the chair next to the radar tech and stared at the display. The *Warrior's* sensor technology was state-of-the-art and was expected to pick up contacts long before any other ship could find them. As he observed the radar screen, the three large blips began to resolve themselves into three separate formations of ships.

"Why isn't the IFF identifying the targets?"

"We're still too far to pick up friendly IDs, sir."

"Very well."

After five days' travel, the *Warrior* was in the middle of the asteroid belt. Nearly all UP ships had been recalled to Mars, so coming upon ships in this area was a surprise.

Gallant marched into the center of the bridge and the OOD immediately vacated the command chair. He sat down and pulled up several screens, giving him the complete picture of all the ship's activities. Satisfied that everything was operating normally, he turned his attention to the contacts. Drumming his fingers on the armrest of the chair he thought,

Could all of these formations be Titans?

The minutes dragged on, and the chatter on the bridge returned to normal. The OOD checked the radar status several times, but the contacts were little changed.

Finally, "Bridge, CIC; we can identify the two nearest ship formations. The closest consists of twelve UP transports heading toward Mars. Its course will intersect and cross ahead of the *Warrior's* at close range. The second formation appears to be UP warships, but we can't identify individual ships yet."

"CIC, bridge," Gallant responded. "Any idea what UP ships are doing in the middle of the asteroid belt with Titans all over the place?"

"Bridge, CIC; There is an NNR mining colony in the area. Our best guess is that this might be a last minute evacuation, sir," said the CIC analyst.

"CIC, bridge; then that second formation could be an escorting task force?"

"Bridge, CIC; affirmative, sir."

"CIC, bridge; what about the third formation trailing behind?"

"Bridge, CIC; my guess is that would be the bad guys, sir."

"Officer of the deck, engage stealth mode," Gallant ordered.

"Engage stealth mode, aye aye, sir."

"Operations, bridge," the OOD said, "Initiate confinement field and bring stealth battery utilization to standard power."

"Bridge, operations; aye aye, sir," responded the operations compartment LPO as he made manual adjustments on his control manifold. The process of creating a confinement field from quark-color charges using their Higgs superconductor battery required a great deal of energy. When the superconductor battery was discharging at the standard rate, the operator proceeded to generate a cloak confinement field around the ship that absorbed all incident particles and emissions, rendering the ship invisible and undetectable.

It took three minutes for the *Warrior* to disappear from the detectable universe.

A few minutes later, CIC identified the first formation of UP ships as twelve transports, and the second UP formation as one battle cruiser and six destroyers. The third group was a large formation of Titan warships chasing the others.

"The battle cruiser is the *Repulse*, sir," reported CIC.

A minute later CIC reported that the Titan force consisted of a cruiser-destroyer squadron totaling thirty-six ships. The *Warrior's* current course would lead them close to the fleeing ships and their pursuers.

Gallant was aware that the war situation had deteriorated to the point that operations within the asteroid belt were risky for any UP ship. Outposts and observation stations were still being abandoned for fear of being cut off and strangled by enemy forces. He saw the evacuation of this mining colony as a measure that should have been undertaken much earlier. The fact that they were using a dozen transports, a battle cruiser, and half a dozen destroyers was evidence of their commitment to see it through, but evidently this operation was a result of reticence and miscalculation. He couldn't be sure if the culprit was Fleet Command, or NNR, or both.

"Fleet Command must've been in agony trying to figure out how to evacuate these colonists," Gallant speculated aloud. "The UP warships are stretched thin trying to defend the colonists and the inner planets. They dispatched a small cover force hoping it would be enough, but events seldom unfold as expected in war, and while you can always hope for salvation, sometimes the enemy gets the upper hand."

"Orders, sir?" the OOD asked.

14

WE FIGHT

"A hell of a way to blunder into a battle—outflanked and outgunned," Gallant complained.

"Could've been worse," quipped Chief Howard.

That bravado might have dissolved Gallant's scowl if he hadn't been watching his tactical display that showed the situation was actually deteriorating.

"Bridge, CIC; It appears that *Repulse* and six destroyers are fighting a rearguard action and have come under fire from the Titans' lead ships."

So far the stealth technology was working; the *Warrior* was undetected, but the ship and its crew were facing their first real challenge. Gallant considered his next move—fight or flight—only one would be right.

Gallant recalled his combat experiences and felt the exhilarating rush of adrenalin as he anticipated the life-or-death gamble he faced. Was this good fortune? Was this an opportunity to distinguish himself and his ship and banish those who perpetually doubted him? Would it matter to them? Or should he steer clear of this engagement and complete his vital mission, a mission Admiral Collingsworth identified as critical to the survival of the United Planets? Could he afford to place such a mission in jeopardy? Could he live with being an uninvolved bystander to what might be a massacre? Could the *Warrior* make a difference? Was he letting his personal concerns cloud his judgment? He needed time to weigh the options before making the decision. He despised himself for the weakness of his indecision. It was reckless to hope that luck would save the convoy and absolve him of responsibility. He hated moments of negative self-reflection when he berated himself. He wasn't sure why he chose to engage in them, but it seemed to be part of his nature to question himself endlessly as if by doing so he would find a revelation to solve his vexing problems. He was never sure it helped, and yet . . . finally . . . in this case, he reached a decision.

With unflinching eyes, Gallant issued a series of rapid-fire orders . . .

"Helm, set course to converge on the convoy."

"Engineering, bridge; ahead full."

"Weapons, bridge; charge the FASER cannon."

"Operations, bridge; increase stealth mode to maximum power."

The *Warrior* converged on the battle space.

"I'm going to CIC," said Gallant.

Roberts stood and announced, "This is Lieutenant Roberts. I have the conn."

In CIC, Gallant stood beside Lieutenant Clay and examined the various displays. His technicians were already analyzing which ships had been damaged. The two made an assessment of the enemy's strength and the *Repulse's* chances to resist.

CIC reported that transports, probably filled with men, women, and children escaping from the colonies, were falling behind, closely pursued by the Titan's lead elements of their formation.

"What's your plan, sir?" Clay asked.

CIC was the heart of the warship's data collection and analysis and the techs were already organizing and processing the battle space information into a form readily usable by their captain. The entire team was bustling about and sharing opinions, each certain he had the answer to whatever issue was addressed. The course, speed, and ID of each ship, friend and enemy alike, was plotted on the large tactical display in the center of the compartment. The display showed the convoy had reached the highest density of the asteroid field.

Gallant asked, "How long until they come within our weapons envelope?"

"The transports and their escorts are heading straight for Mars at maximum speed. The Titans are trailing them. At our current speed, the *Warrior* will intercept them in sixty-one minutes, sir," said Clay.

A tech added, "Captain Caine's *Repulse* has deployed three destroyers, led by the *Ward,* to his starboard and three destroyers, led by the *Fletcher,* to his port. The UP ships navigated through the asteroids while keeping their formation tight. But despite their best efforts, the UP transports were scattering. "

The battle cruiser was the largest ship in the engagement and was armed with eight large anti-ship missile launchers and a dozen fighters with antimissile missiles. The destroyers carried four anti-ship missiles. All the ships had close range lasers and plasma guns.

"How far behind are the Titans?" asked Gallant.

Clay reported, "The leading elements of the Titan force are about thirty minutes behind the convoy and its escort. I'm surprised the Titans are letting individual ships run ahead of the formation. They normally conduct elaborate, well-coordinated maneuvers. The commander of this force is acting as if he's desperate to catch up with our ships despite any battle mismatch."

"The *Repulse* is sweeping back and forth in front of the aliens' course and firing long range missiles at them," said Gallant. "That's disrupting the enemy's advance, and it should allow the transports to extend their lead."

"But, as a consequence," Clay said, "the Titans are catching up to the rearguard. They're acting like a stalking school of sharks, though they are no longer in a disciplined formation. In fact, they look more like a long string with their fastest ships far in front. It looks like they intend to cripple as many ships as they can and leave them for annihilation later."

Gallant scrutinized the radar scope. The pinpoint lights of the ships seemed to diminish in space. His instincts told him there was little he could do, but he was furious and frustrated at his inability to join the action. As the procession of the three formations continued, he wondered,

So much lay behind them; what lay ahead?

"Sir, the *Repulse* has launched a squadron of fighters to help intercept incoming missiles," reported Clay.

The aliens launched their first missile volley, including dozens of large and small missiles. As the missiles approached the UP force, countermeasures were deployed. Decoys and chaff misdirected many of the incoming weapons. Then it was the fighters' turn. They acquired a target and launched their AMM-3 Mongoose antimissile missiles.

"Captain Caine is coordinating maneuvers of his destroyer columns to confuse the enemy," Clay reported. "First, he sends the *Fletcher* group to attack the lead cruisers and fire their missiles. As soon as those three ships begin their return, the second groups of destroyers follow the *Ward* in an attack run. I think it's keeping the Titans confused and off balance."

Despite Caine's tactics, a Titan cruiser was streaming forward, leading a procession of ships each more powerful than the next and, with their greater speed, the aliens were bearing down on the rearguard. Caine tried to parry the Titan tactics by sending the destroyers in to dart and maneuver wildly, but the alien ships were well prepared for that strategy. Nevertheless, the *Repulse* blocked the way, preventing the Titans from getting at the vulnerable transports.

At that critical juncture, Caine ordered the destroyers to launch an all-out counterattack by charging at the Titan ships and launching missiles. Their mission was to protect innocent families. The destroyers fully realized they had little chance of winning against the swarming force of the enemy, but they continued to play their role. Confronted by the superior enemy forces, the UP destroyers launched their missiles and then turned to retreat to the *Repulse*.

As the distance between the rearguard and the Titans decreased, the aliens fired their missiles and scored some hits, damaging nearly all the UP warships. The missiles were armed with multiple warheads, each yielding several megatons of TNT.

The flight time of the UP missiles was a mere seventy seconds. Gallant could see the flashes of the exploding missiles, knowing that every hit was a dagger in the heart of some ship. A few alien missiles detonated near the *Repulse*. The first tremendous shock wave of the explosions pounded that ship. The nuclear warheads damaged the battle cruiser's forward shield and ruptured its forward missile compartment. The communications channels were alive with frantic messages as the ships called for help.

The destroyer *Fletcher*, on the port side of the *Repulse*, directed its small band of destroyers at the leading enemy units. They exchanged laser and plasma fire at close range. The *Fletcher* moved hard to port, readjusting its position to meet enemy fire. The salvos were falling on target, but they did not have enough forces to cover their flanks, so the enemy was moving around them. There was little chance of them escaping unscathed from the Titans' withering fire.

Gallant could make out several destroyers running directly at a Titan cruiser, firing and then running back to the convoy. After taking a hit, one destroyer slowed and fell behind. It became easy prey for the following Titans. The hapless ship struggled to get away, but it was marked by explosions of orange flame until the destroyer finally disappeared in a flash.

The devastating accuracy of the missile fire was disheartening to watch. Another destroyer was hit and became a frantic mess of twisted steel as the explosion could be identified millions of miles away. Consumed by white hot flames and giving off a bright illumination, the ship collapsed in on itself while it burned and died.

The destroyer *Ward* was firing almost blindly. The Titans were finding the range and hitting it with laser and plasma weapons over and over again. The *Ward* was soon consumed by the plasma blasts and disappeared from the scope.

At this distance the high magnification of the telescopic screens brought the destruction into clear view for the *Warrior* to witness. The wreckage of the warships was strewn everywhere. As the minutes ticked by, the pursuit from the Titan ships grew tighter, and Gallant watched as a few surviving warships made it deeper into the asteroid fields and became less visible on the radar scopes.

Gallant was aware that space combat was different than hand-to-hand ground combat. It seemed more antiseptic, and yet death was just as final. The unheard screams of individuals dying from hot plasma burns were as real as a knife plunging into a chest. Whether from flames, shock, shrapnel, shredding armor, burning steel, or vaporization, all ended with the same death rattle.

A Titan cruiser opened fire, and the nearest UP destroyer closed range while maintaining a parallel course. It was joined by two more destroyers, and their shots wreaked havoc on the enemy. The UP force moved its ships counterclockwise to extend the distance between them and the main body of the Titan forces, but that caused sudden chaos in their formation. It enabled the Titan destroyers to move even closer to continue their devastating fire. The battle dragged on into a collection of skirmishes between the widely disbursed ships, each fighting its own hellish battle. The individual captains launched the ships themselves as weapons to try to protect the fleeing civilians.

The attacking Titans split into several divisions with the main force about thirty light seconds ahead of the formation. The overall effect was a large number were closing on what was left of the UP rear guard. Only three destroyers and the badly damaged *Repulse* remained.

The compressed battle space dictated by the aliens' movements resulted in a great deal of damage to the rear guard. However, the Titans were completely disorganized as a result of the combat and the chaotic pursuit and the *Repulse* continued to aggressively threaten the advance of its Titan pursuers.

The forces were separated by over a million miles, a full seven light seconds, and the aliens were able to fire their missiles more effectively because the missile flight time was sixty-four seconds to target. The heavily armored ships with powerful shields could minimize the blast effects of the nuclear-tipped missiles using speed and distance. They were only within the vicinity of explosions for a minuscule fraction of time, but even though most of the blast dissipated into empty space, there was enough heat plasma to do damage to nearby ships.

The Titans fired missile clusters to increase the energy density of their warhead explosions. The tremendous explosions near one of the destroyers knocked it out of action. The missile compartment ruptured and rendered its weapons system useless. The rest of the ships continued. Antimissile missiles from the destroyers were strewn in the path of the remaining missiles.

Gallant was able to distinguish dozens of missiles from the UP warships that appeared to disable or damage several Titan ships. The UP force was putting up a brave fight. He watched as the *Repulse* swung hard to port, changing its course to avoid being an easy target for the Titan missiles. The follow-up missile exchange produced similar results. Ships were being battered and bruised on both sides, but the number of UP ships was being whittled down.

As missile flight time was reduced further, it didn't allow sufficient time to deploy decoys and countermeasures. The general attack was becoming a ragged affair.

The UP force was badly damaged, but the Titan formation no longer exhibited the sharpness it had at first. Gallant saw his old ship, the *Repulse*, taking the brunt of the hits. She was smacked mercilessly with missiles and plasma weapons. She staggered bravely onward until she finally began to slow. The battle of superior numbers was taking its toll.

"Sir, we are five minutes from intercepting the convoy's course," Clay said

The *Repulse* led the last two UP destroyers in a column. They began to engage the enemy to give the convoy a chance to escape. The *Repulse* dodged and weaved never wasting a motion.

During the action the slowest transport had fallen behind the rest of the convoy. It became a target for Titan missiles and suffered a long distance missile hit. As a result, it slowed even more.

"Sir, many of the enemy ships are damaged and withdrawing, but there is one enemy cruiser maneuvering to cut off the damaged transport," reported a tech.

There was little that the damaged *Repulse* could do without abandoning the rest of the convoy.

Damn, Gallant thought.

He strained his eyes, staring at the console and the view screen to evaluate his options.

"Captain, are you going to support the convoy escorts?" Clay's overwrought voice raised the question and challenged Gallant.

Gallant was torn. He wanted to support the *Repulse,* but that might mean exposing the *Warrior* to damage or destruction without completing her mission. He questioned his right to make such a choice. It would be one thing to sacrifice his own life, but would it be right to sacrifice every person in his crew?

He couldn't just watch and let the Titans destroy the damaged transport filled with colonists. The *Warrior* had to save that ship somehow. There must be something he could do without compromising his mission.

Closer and closer the cloaked *Warrior* drew to the unsuspecting Titan ship that was attacking the damaged transport. Gallant worked her into position to stop the enemy before it intercepted the transport. Inch by inch the *Warrior* crept in stealth mode until she was on one side of the transport, and the stalking Titan cruiser was on the other side firing its laser into her.

He had one advantage, one card to play—the FASER cannon.

Gallant came to a fateful decision: *A bold stroke might pay off.*

"Deactivate stealth mode—drop cloak," he ordered.

The bridge crew stared at him with grim faces.

"Deactivate stealth and drop cloak; aye aye, sir," said Howard. A touch of the screen and it was done. The *Warrior* was now exposed. But it was sitting behind the transport and, as a result, it was momentarily shielded from the Titan cruiser's direct line of sight.

In space warfare you can run or fight, but you must choose quickly because you can't hide for long. The enemy will know where you are the moment you fire. Shooting in battle is mostly automated by computers that calculate the best possible firing range and angle.

Currently, the remaining attacking Titans had their attention focused on the *Repulse* and continued to fire at her and the damaged transport. They wanted the *Repulse,* and they wouldn't accept less. As a result, they were ignoring the newly materialized sloop.

"Excuse me, captain," McCall said loudly, "but I am obliged to point out that you are violating our orders and jeopardizing our mission."

Gallant was surprised at her sudden appearance on the bridge. "Yes, I know," he said.

"The admiral's going to skin your hide for this," McCall whispered.

"I'm sure he will. Stand by to fire FASER."

"Let's get them. Mark range. Check bearing," said Clay.

The range was decreasing, and the potential for exposure was increasing.

"Give me the target's range and speed," Gallant ordered.

"Bearing, mark."

"Set."

"Mark."

They were moving into firing range. The cruiser's miscalculation of the situation left it vulnerable. The aiming and firing circuits automatically adjusted for the travel time of several light seconds and angled the cannon to intercept the target when the beam reached it.

"FASER ready, sir."

"Fire!"

The ship shuddered from the powerful cannon.

The flash emanated from the *Warrior* and streaked to its target at the speed of light.

The target practice paid off; the energy beam struck hit the cruiser. He couldn't see the target from the view screen, but CIC reported a hit amidships.

The enemy's engine room erupted, and the cruiser staggered before exploding into a red-orange ball as flammable material within the ship ignited. A great mushroom of white ash and debris was emitted. There was no sound in space, but witnesses to the event felt as if they had heard a monstrous roar.

"We must have hit a magazine," said a tech.

He wasn't trying to eliminate the ship outright; he wanted to cripple it sufficiently to allow them to escape safely.

"Bearing to next cruiser," ordered Gallant, preparing to continue firing, but before he could select a new target CIC reported, "Sir, the Titans appear to be breaking off."

We've done what we can. That's enough.

"Let's not dally. We've done our job. The damaged transport is getting away. The rest of the Titans look like they're slowing down to reorganize their formation. Let's get out of here. Chief Howard, reengage stealth mode."

"Aye aye, sir."

They had already used considerable stealth battery.

"Sir, we're receiving a message from the *Repulse*; it must have picked up our ID transponder."

The message was simple: "Thank you, *Warrior*."

Over the next hour, the rest of the Titan ships gave up the chase, so the UP convoy and its escorts made good their escape.

"Shall I secure from battle stations, sir?"

"Yes."

No sooner had they secured than Gallant sensed the sounds and motions of the ship change.

He hadn't done anything by the book. And while this battle was over, there were more to come. Nevertheless, if there were any lingering doubts among the crew about the *Warrior*, he hoped this had put an end to them.

Bone-tired, Gallant entered his stateroom and collapsed on his bed. He didn't stir for the next six hours.

15

TURNED TO DUST

It took four more days for the *Warrior* to emerge from the asteroid belt, but when it did, Gallant was surprised to witness the Titan armada passing between them and Jupiter. The armada was heading toward its bases on Ganymede, the largest of Jupiter's sixty-three moons, which was in the process of being transformed to make it habitable for the methane-breathing aliens.

Gallant sat in his command chair while his ship approached the planet in stealth mode. Soon Jupiter filled the entire forward view screen. The bridge crew seemed mesmerized by the spectacular image of the gas giant's surface as it provided a picturesque backdrop for the many, many, many Titan warships that stretched from one end of the horizon to the other.

When Gallant had been deployed to Jupiter several years earlier, its moons had hosted thriving colonies. Orbiting satellites and a space station had once serviced hundreds of ships traveling between Jupiter and the inner planets. The Jupiter Station orbited Ganymede and repaired, maintained, and refueled military and commercial ships—many the property of NNR Shipping. The moons included a dozen small pioneer settlements with tens of thousands of colonists each. In total, the planetary system had been home to over half a million colonists living in shelters they had carved out of the various moons rocky surfaces. But the attack by the aliens had laid waste to all of that, leaving only the dust that now circulated within the faint rings of Jupiter.

Although many details of the battle were widely known, the *Warrior's* crew was not prepared for the pitiless evidence before them. They took a good look at what was left of the Jupiter Station—the nearby floating debris was a combination of metal, rocks, and human remains. Awful images of the shattered colonies and the moons devastated by nuclear attack produced a profound impression they would never forget.

Gallant shook off the melancholy thoughts and said aloud, "If anyone ever asks you why we fight, tell them that when someone does unspeakable things to those you care about it's no longer a choice, it's a responsibility."

He was quiet for a moment. Then he added, "Jupiter is now enemy territory."

"Yes, sir," said Roberts.

"As our first act toward reclaiming Jupiter," Gallant continued, "I intend to establish a base of operations. This base will serve two purposes. It will be our hideout where the *Warrior* can recharge her stealth battery, and it will function as a communications relay station."

Gallant and the XO worked in the CIC to evaluate locations for the base.

"How about here, sir?" asked a CIC analyst, pointing to an asteroid cluster near Jupiter's orbit. The asteroid belt was located roughly between the orbits of Mars and Jupiter and included numerous irregularly shaped rocky bodies and minor planets; however, skirting the outer edge of the belt, near the Lagrangian points, were three smaller clusters; the Cybele group, the Hilda family, and the Trojan family. The last was closest to Jupiter's orbit. Those asteroids included objects larger than one kilometer wide and were as numerous as within the asteroid belt. The analyst identified a cluster of large asteroids that formed a natural pocket, a harbor-like configuration, within the Trojan family.

"Yes, that might do," said Gallant. "It affords the best prospect for a hidden base. It's large enough to block radar detection as well as any direct visibility from Titan ships traveling near Jupiter. The *Warrior* could hide between the kilometer-sized rocks while recharging her stealth batteries."

"In addition," Robert's said, "it has several large mountainous outcroppings and cavernous valleys that could shelter and hide a communication relay station on its surface. We could construct and supply the station by shuttlecraft."

"Excellent," said Gallant.

The *Warrior* slid into position behind the Trojan rocks to recharge her stealth batteries. The stealth device used a quark color-charge superconducting field to cloak the ship and render it undetectable. The color charge battery had to be recharged every forty-eight hours to remain at full strength.

A shuttle was sent to the surface of a large asteroid in the Trojan family with supplies and equipment. A two-man team constructed a relay station and thermionic radioisotope power plant. In addition, one of the *Warrior's* three remote-controlled drones was left there for future operations. The communication relay station was designed to transmit and receive signals utilizing the radioisotope power supply along with a large directional antenna. A tiny, almost invisible satellite was placed in orbit with a receiving antenna and a tightly focused laser transmission beam. Using the passive satellite enhanced the overall coverage, range, and capacity of the relay network.

When the *Warrior* was further in space, it could send data to the collection satellite. The ultrahigh frequency communication satellite would then relay the data to the surface unit that would retransmit it to Mars using its stronger nuclear power plant. The directional antenna would require much less transmission power. In addition, a monitoring telescope was placed with its focus constantly on the Jupiter moon bases in order to keep records of ships coming and going after the *Warrior* left for Saturn.

Since it was relatively easy to send a tight directional laser beam from Jupiter to Mars, the relay station would be a great asset. Unfortunately, Mars could not send a similar laser beam to the *Warrior* for two reasons: First, the Mars command would not know an exact intercepting position to reach the *Warrior*; and second, although Mars did have a prearranged emergency site, command felt that sending messages to Jupiter or Saturn would arouse Titan suspicions and alert to the fact that some UP assets were in the area, even if they couldn't read the message itself.

Once the *Warrior* left for Saturn, Gallant could set up another nuclear-powered communications satellite to send data to that relay station. He would have liked to place more monitors and satellites, but he had a limited supply.

"Communications officer, how about doing the honors and giving us a name for this base?" Gallant asked.

"Gee, sir. I thought that was obvious . . . 'Helen,' of course," Gabriel responded.

Gallant had to smile, and the CIC analysts laughed out loud.

"A romantic gesture, Gabriel, but I think after all his observations and contributions related to Jupiter, 'Galileo' would be more appropriate," said Gallant and, as captain, he had the last word.

It took only one day to complete the construction and testing of Base Galileo, after which Gallant decided to reconnoiter the alien bases around Jupiter's moons.

16

FRIENDLY VISIT

It was not the custom in the fleet for a female officer to visit her captain alone in his cabin, but McCall did not observe this rule. After a single light knock, she opened Gallant's cabin door and entered. Without the appearance of haste or embarrassment, she sat down on his cot. With moist lips, smiling eyes, and a sureness of bearing, she exuded a mysterious beauty.

"This ship is simply too small for you to continue to avoid me, Henry," she said.

Gallant remained seated at his desk and took inventory of the numerous upsetting reactions he was experiencing in response to her uninvited presence. To his amazement, she sat in front of him brazenly staring at him—as if she would wait forever for him to suitably acknowledge her. He started to rise in protest, but immediately relented and sat down once more, resolved to the situation as if he had half expected it.

"Henry, your vacillating ruminations are a source of great amusement to me," she laughed.

He spoke at last, "Am I really such a captivating subject?"

She laughed again, more fulsomely this time. Shaking her head, she said, "Nothing is more resilient than the male ego."

Gallant shifted in his seat. "I'm not sure I'm comfortable with that portrait."

She continued to stare at him while she tapped her fingers rhythmically on the top of the desk. Gallant remained mesmerized by the overall effect. His face grew rosy under her scrutiny. He felt self-conscious, because, admittedly, he still had no idea how to cope with her—either as an agent or as a woman.

Finally, suppressing his internal upheaval, he asked, "What can I do for you?"

Her remarkable blues eyes met his as she drew a deep breath.

She said, "Your question is deliciously troubling."

"Troubling? I merely asked what you require."

"I would've thought my wishes were clear," she said, as if she was prepared to complicate his day.

Flustered once more, he thought,

She clearly isn't interested in getting to the point.

Under different circumstances, he might have enjoyed the flirtatious banter, but he was afraid things were already becoming problematic.

Distracted by a sound coming from the hallway, McCall turned away. When she turned back, her smile was gone.

She said, "Captain, let me speak frankly. This mission will be difficult and dangerous. You and I will need to work closely together."

She paused. Then with an earnest expression, she added, "I've been fortunate to learn a great deal about you from reports on your recent adventures."

Putting her hand on his, she said, "Will you spare me a few minutes now to learn more about the man behind the deeds?"

Gallant remained wary, but said, "If you will reciprocate by letting me know a little about you."

Suddenly the atmosphere in the minute cabin was transformed.

McCall spoke rapidly with a sense of delight. "Oh yes, please. Let me start. I'll tell you a story," she said, her eyes shining with pleasure. "As a child, I often stood on a hillside where I could look across the horizon for a sign of a ship landing. I would wait long hours for many days. I never grew weary, or concerned about time, because eventually I would see the figure of a man at a great distance. When he approached, I would run and hide in the forest, to wait some more—to tease him. I would hear him calling out for me, 'Julie Anne? Julie Anne?' He would call and call. This pleased me and gave me a sense of gratification after all of my patient waiting. And when, finally, I pounced out of the shadows at him, we would embrace. Then I would confide all my dreams, my hopes, and my fears. I held nothing back. Each time he returned I took it as a fulfillment of my faith in him—the faith of a daughter for her father."

Gallant witnessed her joy in telling the story and was about to speak when McCall continued, "When you're young, you ask many, many questions. Why do things fall? Why is the sky blue? Children are enormously curious that way. And the one who provides the answers becomes the child's fountain of enlightenment. For me, it was my father. Throughout my life, he was my mentor. As a fleet officer, he eventually inspired me to serve in the fleet myself. He was the driving motivation for my career."

Gallant was impressed with her candor.

McCall's voice grew deep and sad as she said, "When Jupiter Station was destroyed my father was one of the many casualties, just like Lieutenant Clay's family. That's something I share with him."

After a few minutes, her mood once more lifted and she offered an alternative topic of conversation. "Tell me about Alaina."

Gallant said, "During my mission at Tau Ceti, Alaina Hepburn became president of the planet, Elysium."

"I'm not interested in her politics. I want you to tell me about her."

Gallant hesitated before revealing, "She lost her parents at an early age, as did I. She grew up a little wild. She's a free spirit—passionately independent and fiercely determined to help her people."

McCall said, "Good for her. Now tell me about your relationship with her. Does she make you happy?"

"Yes, she does, actually."

"Are you in a committed relationship?"

Gallant had to reflect on that question since he didn't actually know the answer himself.

McCall continued, "You should be careful. Her political agenda may not be perfectly aligned with the United Planets. You could find yourself in a compromised situation."

"I thought you weren't interested in her politics?"

"Touché."

Then she took a deep breath and asked, "What are your expectations for this mission?"

Once more he hesitated, but she waited, looking at him expectantly.

Gallant confided, "Those who serve in the fleet are prepared to make sacrifices to fulfill their mission. My sacrifices have involved personal injuries." He paused struggling with his sense of discretion, but he found himself saying, "But as captain of this ship, I'm responsible to balance the sacrifice of my entire crew against the needs of our mission."

He paused once more and, staring straight ahead, he said, "My greatest fear is failing them."

McCall asked quietly, "Failing? How? By demanding too much?" She paused. Then she whispered, "Or not enough?"

He looked at her, not speaking for a long moment fearing he had divulged too much of himself. He had not intended to speak so frankly to an SIA agent, but it struck him it was a tribute to her skills as an interrogator.

Gallant stood and said, "Thank you for coming by, commander. I've found our conversation enlightening. If you'll excuse me now, I'm needed on the bridge.

17

LOOKING IN

From several million kilometers distance, the *Warrior* managed a bird's-eye view of the alien's main base around Jupiter. The base itself was built on Ganymede's surface, but an orbiting shipyard and space station were being constructed in a surrounding cluster of rocks, creating a cocoon-like space harbor.

Operating in stealth mode the *Warrior* approached the outer edge of the harbor and began cautiously conducting a spiral search to map the interrelated defenses. The crew was excited to penetrate deep into Titan territory.

"We've reached the harbor's maximum missile range, sir," said the officer of the deck.

"Very well," said Gallant. "We'll alter course in a few minutes. Gather as much data as possible."

"Aye aye, sir," responded CIC.

McCall was hard at work with several CIC techs collecting information about defenses, missile batteries, ships, and base facilities. They noted a space station under construction and the several hundred ships in orbit around Ganymede. Jupiter's moons were alive, and there were numerous ships traveling among them.

At the outer edges of the harbor, the picket ships patrolled between satellite sensor arrays. Drones moved between the various stations for some unknown purpose. Since the *Warrior's* trajectory passed close to many of those listening posts, they would experience a real test of the stealth technology.

A Titan picket ship lumbered close but failed to discover the *Warrior*. The satellite sensor array likewise failed.

Gallant thought, *Our stealth system is doing well.*

The navigator said, "We're coming up on a course change."

"Closest approach will occur ninety seconds after we alter course, sir," reported the sensor tech.

"That's inside their effective missile range, sir," said the OOD.

"I hope our intelligence estimates are accurate," said Gallant.

"Me too, skipper," said Roberts.

"Very well. Execute course change."

"Aye aye, sir."

The CIC reported that one of the picket ships altered course in the general direction of the *Warrior*.

The agile *Warrior* was prepared to open fire from every laser and plasma battery if it came to that, but she was a small ship, and her chances of surviving a serious engagement were unrealistic. Despite a moment of concern, the picket moved away, once again failing to detect the *Warrior*.

"We're slipping through, sir," reported the sensor tech.

They were now at the threshold of the harbor mouth and had a splendid view of the inner bastion.

"We'll change course while observing their ships," said Gallant. "Mr. Roberts, come left ten degrees, set course 122, mark three."

"Aye aye, sir."

"CIC, bridge; give me a count of enemy shipping inside the harbor."

After a few minutes, CIC reported, "Bridge, CIC; We can make out 324 warships, sir. Three dozen battle cruisers are in orbit near the space station along with 144 cruisers and a like number of destroyers. There are numerous civilian vessels, and there are 144 transports, mining ships, and cargo ships scattered across the rear area. The remainder includes smaller craft shuttling between the large vessels and the base. There are several markers we can use to identify this region. The beacon marker to starboard will be useful to take our bearings."

"Bridge, CIC; cruiser close to starboard."

"That will be the on-station duty cruiser," Roberts observed.

"Yes. Let's test our stealth capability by seeing how close we can come," said Gallant. He checked the console, scanning the navigation information available to them and examining their options. On the one hand, Gallant wanted to test their capabilities; on the other, he didn't want to press his luck. Constant observation and testing would improve their information gathering geometrically as well as their abilities to avoid detection.

"The duty ship seems to be heading in our general direction," said Roberts, sweat dripping down his forehead.

"Bridge, engineering; captain, you requested to be notified when the stealth battery charge depleted to 20 percent, sir. We've reached that point."

"Engineering, bridge; Very well," said Gallant.

"I think we've come close enough," Gallant said to the bridge crew. "Let's back off slowly, Mr. Roberts. It's time to head back to Base Galileo for a recharge."

※

The following day, Gallant decided to act even more boldly. While he believed in extensive planning, he expected any individual plan would have to evolve during an actual operation. A successful leader usually is required to evolve with the changing circumstances. Forecasting a variety of scenarios in the planning stages helped him prepare for rapid changes during an actual operation. So to help him prepare for surprises, he called for a roundtable discussion in the wardroom to cajole his officers into offering their speculative opinions.

The plan they devised was for the *Warrior* to stay in standard stealth mode and orbit Ganymede while the small two-man Wasp used its own stealth capabilities to venture deep into the harbor itself.

Gallant and Gabriel would fly the Wasp into the heart of the enemy stronghold and evaluate the defenses in detail. The small craft was configured for a moderate stealth level with prolonged endurance by minimizing its speed.

The CIC would track the Wasp and monitor the sensory collection of information. When the mission was completed, the Wasp would return to the selected rendezvous point.

"Mr. Roberts," Gallant said, "I'm sorry, but you're to remain aboard ship; the circumstances dictate that Mr. Gabriel accompany me. He's the communications officer and has undergone the specialized stealth training for the Wasp." Smiling, he added, "Besides, a command-rank officer must remain aboard the *Warrior*."

"I'm sure it couldn't be otherwise, sir," said the XO.

He sounded philosophical, but he also sounded disappointed. It was the perverse logic of war such that Roberts was bitter at not participating in a highly dangerous mission while Gallant apologized because he was facing that very peril. And Gallant had to admit he was not happy to leave his ship in the hands of another while he was away.

"Do you have any last-minute questions?" asked Gallant.

"No sir."

"Then I'll go to the flight deck and join Gabriel. I'll let you know when we're ready for launch."

"Yes, sir."

Upon reaching the flight deck, Gallant found Gabriel already strapped into position. Chief Howard was standing beside the hatch of the Wasp: "You needn't worry, young man. The skipper will run this mission like clockwork. You'll be in and out before you've had a chance to worry. Remain calm and follow his instructions. He knows his job." Howard then gave him a thumbs-up.

Visibly brightened, the midshipman nodded enthusiastically: "You can count on me, chief." And he returned the thumbs-up.

"I know I can, Gabe," and the crusty CPO smiled.

Watching the two of them, Gallant thought,

The youngest and the oldest are natural allies.

He scooted into the command chair and strapped in. Pulling the neural interface over his head, he connected to the AI flight controls and began interfacing with the main controls and sensors. He started the Wasp's engines by visualizing the process. While the neural interface worked great for small craft, Gallant hoped that someday it could be applied to larger ships such as the *Warrior*.

Gallant looked at Gabriel expectantly.

"Ready, sir."

"Bridge, Wasp; request permission to launch."

"Wasp, bridge; you are cleared for launch," Roberts said.

As Gallant launched the craft, the acceleration forced the two passengers against their seats as they departed the *Warrior*.

"Activate stealth mode," ordered Gallant.

"Aye aye, sir," said Gabriel as he activated his neural interface and connected to the ship's AI controls. He formed a mental image of the stealth controls and began powering them up. With both men tied into the AI system, they were able share some of their mental processes and hear each other's active thoughts.

As they approached the Ganymede base under stealth mode, Gallant thought, *Give me a detailed count of enemy shipping, their positions, and their operational status.*

Gabriel thought, *Yes, sir. I'll get a fix now.*

Gabriel appeared nervous undertaking this first significant responsibility. However, he was making every effort to be alert and do his job. Gallant efficiently performed the major requirements of the mission, but also began to train Gabriel in some of the simpler aspects of the ship's operations. He gave Gabriel instructions and let him try various procedures.

They were both getting the feel of the ship and found it a pleasure to fly. Gallant found Gabriel to be a quick study and, though he made mistakes, he didn't repeat them, a quality Gallant appreciated.

They continued operating for several hours, all the while collecting data on the inner defenses.

Gallant was able to sneak into one of the fleet operations areas and watch training and mock exercises. He gathered a wealth of information about the Titans' military capabilities and operations.

Though tired, Gallant was satisfied with the mission, and he was glad to return to his *Warrior* once their stealth battery charge reached 20 percent. They returned to the rendezvous point and uploaded their data into the *Warrior's* main computer.

When the craft was recovered, Howard personally checked every system to ensure it would be fully operational for the next mission.

༄

Gallant reviewed the communication messages they had intercepted from the general radio broadcasts. To translate them, he relied on his neural AI interface to draw from a database of concepts and relationships. Even the simplest statements were vexing to reach an interpretation and he had to reevaluate his translation on many occasions.

Thinking in imagery and sensory perceptions was difficult enough, but translating those thoughts to meaningful words and numbers was a challenge. He tried to use number theory to unravel the hidden meaning of the complex sensory relationships. Gallant found that one asset was repetition; many of the phrases used by the aliens featured repeated images that he could pick out. Everything he tried was laborious, and he had to start over when he found himself in contradictions. The most difficult translations involved self-references in which the aliens referred to what they believed to be true. It was vital he uncovered the meaning of the messages correctly, or the intelligence he sent to Mars would mislead the high command.

During the course of his endeavors, he wondered what the aliens' poetry would be like—if they had such a thing.

18

SHADOW

What followed were busy days as the *Warrior* cruised Titan territory, and the Wasp peeked into the harbor. Together they compiled a detailed list of warships and their deposition as well as their refueling and patrolling patterns. They soon learned the shipping traffic patterns and came to understand some of the industrial capacity and accumulate population statistics. The CIC developed some preliminary estimates for the industry and population infrastructure for each of Jupiter's moons. It kept a status display showing the time-sensitive information about energy emissions for different sites that indicated industrial and mining operations at hundreds of locations. McCall was startled to find that the population estimates indicated over half a million Titans were already living in various colonies on the moons of Jupiter.

On a regular basis, the mission sent a directional laser signal back to Base Galileo, and the base relayed the data to Mars. So far their efforts had learned of the physical disposition of the enemy, but what was needed next was hard intelligence to learn about their plans. But Gallant was the only person who could understand what the Titans were saying over their open communication channels so progress was slow.

When the *Warrior* wasn't recharging her battery or conducting observations, the crew ran drills. Gallant surmised that rather than being a source of complaint, the demanding schedule was a source of pride for the crew. The members of the crew felt a sense of accomplishment by doing something truly important. As a result, they were developing a collective personality and a fiercely aggressive spirit.

On occasion, Gallant passed through the crew's mess to catch a few moments of their unguarded conversations, hoping to gain some firsthand insight into their morale.

Between meals the crew filled their spare time with social activities such as queuing up for haircuts, trading food rations, or boasting of past exploits. There was a lot of good-natured ribbing and plenty of talk about what they planned to do after the mission. Home was a major theme. The crew members who had combat experience were reluctant to share their war stories; mostly they shrugged off their experience and said, "You'll find out soon enough."

One day while Gallant was inspecting the weapons compartment with Lt. Clay, he asked him his opinion on what risks he thought were appropriate for the Wasp's next excursion.

Clay showed his keen desire to get at the enemy and said, "It's good for this ship to have an aggressive leader. I hope you're willing to exploit every opportunity."

Gallant said cautiously, "Aggression is good, but there can be no place for carelessness. Everything needs to be well thought out." Clay possessed a bloodthirsty desire to attack the enemy. He had expressed his sense that this was a personal war because of the massacre of his family on Jupiter Station. The crew was sympathetic with his point of view and let him rant and vent his anger, but Gallant saw such behavior as something he would have to monitor. Their conversation was interrupted by a call from the bridge.

When Gallant reached the bridge, the OOD said, "The duty cruiser is on our starboard quarter and crossing ahead of us at close range, sir."

Gallant decided not to change course. The duty ship passed close by, but ignominiously failed to raise the alarm. Satisfied, Gallant then changed course. To his surprise, the duty cruiser took an intercepting vector toward the *Warrior*. The movement alarmed everyone on the bridge.

"Verify that our stealth equipment is functioning properly," ordered Gallant.

"Everything checks normal, sir," the OOD reported.

"I don't like it. Mark that bearing."

"Aye aye, sir. Bearing, mark. Bearing, mark."

The CIC repeated the bearing over several minutes and plotted an exact course for their opponent. The *Warrior* was hurtling further and further away from the moon, giving them more room to operate. But the duty cruiser continued to shadow their movements. The cat-and-mouse game continued for several more minutes; all the while Gallant was wondering why this particular vigilant guard was not calling for reinforcements.

"We better lose our shadow before our battery gets much lower," said Roberts.

Gallant ordered the stealth mode status rechecked. Gallant then changed course again and again, but the duty cruiser changed course likewise. He ordered a complete examination of the ship's emissions to test for any leakage. They had to find whatever signal the cruiser was tracking. Increasingly, it seemed only a matter of time before they would fall afoul of this enemy. The duty cruiser moved closer with each course change. They were now in a race that the *Warrior* couldn't afford to lose.

"Time for a course change again, sir?" Roberts asked tentatively.

"I think we'll wait a little longer," said Gallant. "The duty cruiser's commander is no fool. He's observed something that has made him suspicious, and he's investigating before raising the alarm. The question is what did he observe and how long will he keep his suspicions to himself?"

"She's gaining on us sir," said the OOD.

The *Warrior* had lost some of her precious lead, and all the while her stealth power was falling dangerously low.

Gallant was becoming concerned . . . *What does that ship see?*

It was becoming an exhausting struggle. The shadowy shape was still on their tail. Back-and-forth Gallant maneuvered his ship trying to shake his determined pursuer, hoping to convince them that they were chasing a ghost signal of some kind.

He maintained a constant course for an extended period, and the gap to the duty ship widened. The seconds passed like minutes as the *Warrior* plunged further into space with every crew member feeling the stress.

Gallant stood from his command chair and returned to the back of the bridge where he began pacing. Suppose, he thought, he was compelled to fight a close action against this cruiser. What were his chances? He wasn't sure his shields would hold or that his weapons would be powerful enough to stand them in good stead. The odds of a cruiser against a sloop ordinarily would have been inconceivable, but the *Warrior* had already proved she was no ordinary ship. He shook himself from the black mood foisted on him by the mysterious shadow, but there was no time for introspection; he had to find some creative way to rid themselves of this dogged follower.

"The stealth battery is 90 percent depleted," Roberts reported. "I don't think we can continue this course of action much longer."

Gallant fixed his gaze on Roberts. His unwavering stare forced Roberts to turn away.

"Is there a large asteroid we can use for cover?" Gallant asked the sensor tech.

"We're in the main section of Jupiter's largest rings, but we're well away from the larger rocks, sir."

They changed course once more and headed toward Base Galileo. They waited to see what the Titan commander would do. The duty cruiser continued to move closer.

Gallant ordered several hands to deploy a small decoy drone whose signal might mislead the duty cruiser.

"Standby to change course to starboard. Deploy the decoy," ordered Gallant. He had to fool the Titan commander who already had proven he was no fool.

"Decoy away, sir."

"Change course to starboard."

As the *Warrior* separated from the decoy, she began increasing the distance from the cruiser. The decoy had attracted the picket ship; it looked as if it were preforming its function.

Then Gallant increased speed to make good their escape, but at that point the duty cruiser once again adopted an intercepting course.

"Reduce speed to ahead one-third. Set course 270, mark two," Gallant ordered.

At that power setting, the *Warrior's* engines were applying exactly enough thrust to counterbalance Jupiter's gravity, putting the ship in a stationary orbit around the gas giant so it would travel in tandem with the rocks in the ring.

Then the cruiser exhibited confusion. It had lost whatever signal it was following. The cruiser began a circular search pattern, apparently trying to find the *Warrior* again. The duty cruiser then fired its laser randomly, perhaps hoping for a lucky shot.

Gallant was resolute to find a solution to his shadow but, frustrated at not finding a reason for the *Warrior's* exposure, he changed course toward Base Galileo once more: "Increase speed to ahead, two-thirds."

Again, the cruiser took an intercepting vector course toward the *Warrior*.

"Aha!" said Gallant. "Helm, ahead one-third. Maintain a stationary orbit within the ring."

The noise level on the bridge rose appreciably. For the first time during the episode, the crew chatter became noticeable.

"Captain, that cruiser will be down on us in a matter of minutes," said Roberts. There was no mistaking the tension in his voice.

Gallant remained silent and waited. The bridge became stone silent once more.

After two minutes, the cruiser turned and adopted a circular search pattern once more. After several more minutes it had moved far from the *Warrior*.

"It's the rings," Gallant said. "We're leaving a turbulence wake from our motion through the rings, even in stealth mode. The cruiser has been investigating that unusual turbulence. Once we stopped accelerating, our wake diminished. It didn't disappear altogether, but our movement carried us forward balancing against Jupiter's gravity. Fortunately, our turbulence diminished."

With every minute the *Warrior* pulled further and further from the cruiser's reach, allowing them to make good their escape.

"Mr. Roberts, take us back to Base Galileo—slowly."

"Aye aye, sir."

"Helm, ahead one third. Set course 020, mark one."

"Aye aye, sir."

Gallant listened to the change in the chatter around him.

"That was spooky . . ."

"Hell, that was closer than I want to think . . ."

"There's a war on, you know . . ."

"Yeah, so I heard . . ."

"You know what I think? I think . . ."

". . . then we picked up these signals in CIC . . ."

"Well, if you're so smart, what was all that stuff about wakes in the rings, huh?"

"We were lucky . . ."

The chin-wagging kept up for quite a while.

Gallant monitored the ship's wake as it left the sparse rings of Jupiter and entered a void. He had learned a lesson: Operating within the planet's rings caused the dust particles to produce a turbulence that revealed their motion. They needed to devise a plan to avoid that issue. He was tempted to stay away from the rings altogether, but even if they sent all the data they had already collected to Mars, their mission required much more.

"We have to find a way of traveling safely through the rings," Clay said egging his captain on.

Gallant thought, *I have an idea on how we can fool the Titans.*

19

BUGGED

Gallant awoke with a delicious sense of well-being, eager to start the day. He sat upright on his cot, still bathed in the satisfaction of shaking off the *Warrior's* shadow. His body was invigorated, and his mind overflowed with plans. He threw his legs over the side, leaned forward, and let his momentum carry him out of bed. He splashed water on his face and washed his mouth out. Then with a light heart, he showered and donned a fresh uniform. When he was ready for breakfast, a wave of temptation hit him—he had an impulse to treat himself to something special.

While the ship's synthetics were sufficient to sustain life, after a few weeks they played havoc with morale. He considered supplementing his normal breakfast repast with some items of real flavor and taste. Opening his personal locker, he rifled through a small refrigerator that stored the few real foodstuffs allotted to him. They included a few dairy items and several pieces of dried meats that he intended to ration over the course of the mission. He knew that, soon enough, it would be gone, and then he would be subjected to an endless stream of artificial food. Nevertheless, he was determined to enjoy this day.

He took out two crackers, one-tenth ounce of cheese, a thimble of jam, and a capsule of real egg concentrate—priceless commodities to someone 300 million kilometers from home. He then closed the locker, and carried his treasures to the empty wardroom where he spread the food out on the table. While he activated a heating element and cooked the egg concentrate, he pressed a button to activate the coffee dispenser. Soon he was pouring himself a steaming hot cup of synth-coffee. He took two preliminary sips and grimaced at the bitter flavor. He tasted the cheese, and despite finding it salty, he spread a healthy portion on one of his crackers and then covered the other with jam. Pleased with himself for his culinary enterprise, he wolfed the cooked egg and crackers down with several large gulps of synth-coffee. Throwing discretion to the wind, he swallowed a second cup. After a moment he muttered, "A poor substitute for planet-side cooking." But after a moment's reflection, he reconsidered: "Still, it's better than the usual imitations."

Satisfied with his start to the day, he felt compelled to make a quick tour of the ship's spaces to reassure himself that all was well aboard the *Warrior*.

He left his cabin and toured the ship, ending his trek in the CIC.

Looking over the data collection results they had produced so far, Gallant wondered, *Are we ready to take on more risk?*

"I think it's time we carry out our first communication tapping operation," said Gallant, challenging the techs.

"What do you have in mind, sir?"

"Some delicate and sneaky operations."

The war had become more than missiles and lasers; it was eavesdropping and sabotage and anything else that could disrupt the enemy's effort. Special operations were normally kept secret in locked drawers behind closed doors, and they were assigned to knowledgeable veterans—assignments that required steely nerves and quick reflexes. Their success was a compelling testimony to the courage and ingenuity of the clandestine agents carrying them out. Yet the exigencies of war called upon novices Gallant and Gabriel to play their first espionage roles.

They began planning a bugging operation. They decided to tap the main communication junction box on Ganymede. Once a tap was in place, they could collect messages and military orders being transmitted to and from Titan ships around Jupiter. Since the aliens didn't believe the humans could understand Titan communication, they made no attempt to encrypt or codify their messages. That was lucky because it meant Gallant wouldn't have to decrypt or decode the intercepts.

The *Warrior* carried special electrical bugging devices capable of attaching to and penetrating the electronic signals to record the Titans' communications. The greatest problem was getting the Wasp close to the Titans' communication base on the moon's surface. When they reached the location using the Wasp, they would perform an Extravehicular Activity (EVA) and land on the planet in order to insert a tapping device on the communication junction box. They would also plant explosives to destroy the devices if they were ever discovered.

Worry was constant on a frontline spy mission, and Gallant watched how the crew reacted to the youngest officer on board as he prepared for the dangerous mission. There were 126 highly skilled crew members on the *Warrior*, but there was something about Gabriel that inspired the crew to rally around him. His youthful sense of duty coupled with a good-humored, friendly disposition seemed to draw them in. This was a young man they could stand next to and be proud of as he undertook one of the most dangerous operations of the war—slipping into enemy territory and eavesdropping. It was a mission no one had ever dared undertake. No other intelligence operation had embraced so many levels of technology integration coupled with human resources on such a far-reaching mission. In silence and stealth, they would have to creep into the enemy's most sensitive areas to conduct their operation. There was only one good way to conduct such a mission—don't get caught.

In the cold and dark of space, the Wasp faced hazards worse than those of traditional military men in open warfare. Of course, there was always the fear of detection inside enemy territory. The catastrophes that could befall them would mean they might never see home again. The details of their mission were closely held by the top UP admirals, so their efforts—successful or not—might never be known. The risk of it all was increased by the frantic need to have an impact on the war as quickly as possible. They could end up anonymous men in a silent service. Or they might have a vital impact on war planning if they could obtain useful intelligence of the enemy's intentions.

Gallant and Gabriel launched the Wasp and headed for Ganymede. Eavesdropping equipment had been crammed into the over-stuffed ship. They operated the craft deftly and found a place to land on Ganymede near what they hoped, based upon CIC's extensive analysis of the Titans' infrastructure, was the main communication junction box. The SIA equipment on board the Wasp would help them snatch military intelligence from electronic communications. If the mission went as planned, the *Warrior* would be conducting many more operations such as this.

The cramped quarters of the Wasp's steel shell produced fumes and odors that were hard to completely erase, though its two occupants were so intent on their jobs they hardly noticed. The recycling systems for water, oxygen, and other minerals continued nonstop. Comfort was one thing, but staying alive was the main goal, and that required them to stay quiet, stay hidden, and above all, stay alert.

"Were we detected?" asked Gabriel as they landed the Wasp near their selected site.

"I don't know yet," said Gallant.

Once the ship touched down their stealth field collapsed, and they were no longer cloaked. Only the natural camouflage of the surrounding hills protected them.

"Are any ships coming in this direction?" asked Gallant.

"No, sir. Should we get closer to the junction box?"

"Closer? We're practically in their back pocket as it is. How much closer?" There was little room for error.

"I don't know, sir."

"This doesn't feel right. There's no place to hide here. We're too exposed," said Gallant. They took off and moved the Wasp to what they hoped was a better location with more cover.

"The best we can hope for is a semi-protected environment while we're on our operation," said Gallant.

The two men exited the Wasp and began walking, bouncing, and hopping in the low gravity. They wore skin-tight suits that entirely enclosed their bodies including their heads. They also had short-term oxygen capsules that allowed them to breathe for several hours.

There was a chance this would all lead to disaster, so Gallant spent a few minutes clearing his mind.

He found the communication transmission equipment where they planted the bugging device. Doubts and worries were chased away before he began crawling along the outer hub of the communication junction box. Soon they collected a few transmissions as a test to see if everything was functioning normally. Gallant boldly stepped out from the shadows and planted a briefcase-sized bomb at the base of the communication junction box so only he could recover the equipment.

Unfortunately, the bugging equipment failed. The messages were garbled and unreadable. Gallant had to remove it. There is nothing as maddening as bringing your ship millions of kilometers across space, training your crew, and working endless hours to get into a difficult and dangerous position to execute your mission, only to fail because of some inexplicable equipment malfunction.

They returned to the Wasp with the flawed equipment and took off.

When they were back aboard the *Warrior*, Roberts said, "You've got to be outraged to undergo a high-risk mission like this and then find faulty equipment," as he controlled his frustrations.

"That damn piece of junk," said Chief Howard, not even attempting to conceal his fury. He stared at the equipment, incredulous that it could have malfunctioned so completely.

"We've got to find the problem and get it corrected before we can mount another bugging operation," Gallant said with a frown.

"This equipment needs to be planted and retrieved after it has collected data. Then we have to repeat the process over and over again on a regular basis. It will never be a viable operation if it's constantly breaking down. It's crazy. We can't be running in and out like a subway. We're sure to get caught. You can't chance it, sir," Roberts concluded.

The atmosphere of tension grated on Gallant and the CIC analysts. This entire operation was like a blind man feeling in the dark, trying to make sense of what his fingers told him.

As the communications officer, Gabriel was directly responsible for the bugging equipment. He studied the online tech manual for two days straight until he was able to find the problem. The device had not been properly aligned and calibrated in the shipyard despite the shipyard check-off signatures the equipment carried.

Working without rest for eight hours straight and armed with Gabriel's findings, Chief Howard and several techs managed to implement a fix and adjusted the bugging device with a makeshift calibration tool the chief built from scratch.

"Thanks to Mr. Gabriel," Howard said, "we can now have confidence in the bugging devices, but we will have to make adjustments and recalibrations to every bugging device on board before we deploy them. This should have been done properly by the shipyard before we left."

Gallant also blamed the shipyard for not doing a thorough job, but he held his tongue.

Later that day they repeated their excursion to Ganymede and left a functioning recording device.

A few days later they retrieved the recorder's data and found it had performed perfectly.

They were finally ready to conduct regular bugging operations. It was the need for stealth more than anything that convinced them to follow their current line of operations by putting the eavesdropping equipment close to the main communication terminal.

After several excursions they accumulated a significant amount of information about warship operations, but nothing critical had been discovered.

Because of his successful excursions, the wardroom gave the young midshipman a nickname. They began calling him 'Gabe' and treated him like their own personal good luck charm. They started thinking of him as the ship's golden boy.

20

REVISITED

Gallant stood before McCall's stateroom door, poised to knock, yet hesitant to do so. He sorted through his thoughts and attempted to organize his ideas. Finally, he steeled himself and rapped loudly several times.

"Enter," said a muffled voice from within.

He opened the door and threw an uneasy glance inside before stepping into the sparse room. Suddenly he felt himself, not unreasonably, second-guessing his decision to interrogate an SAI agent.

McCall was seated on the lone chair in the room. She looked up at him with a puzzled expression. Leaning back, she let the leather upholstered chair rest against the bulkhead while she crossed her arms and legs—presenting a distinctly frosty welcome. Nevertheless, she managed a weak smile.

"Come in, captain."

"Thank you. I hope I'm not disturbing you," he said in a quiet tone as he appraised her mood. "Can you spare a few minutes?"

McCall's expression appeared neither hospitable nor hostile as she replied, "Of course. Please be seated."

Gallant sat on the only space available—the end of her bed.

"I'm sorry to intrude upon your free time, but there are a few issues I would like to discuss with you and I thought it would be better to address them in private."

"Oh?" she said pleasantly enough, but her eyes revealed that she was unhappy at being placed on the defensive by Gallant's surprise visit.

"You've expressed some concern about my translation of recent Titan messages. I wanted to confer with you about them."

"You're referring to several messages, that when placed together, imply a strategic operation may be underway."

"Exactly," he said leaning forward.

"That's one possibility," she said. Shaking her head, she added, "but I'm worried about jumping to conclusions. We'll have to get much greater detail to confirm it."

Now that he had committed himself, Gallant spoke rapidly, "I think there is a thread within the Titan orders that show the intent to move the entire armada deep into the asteroid belt in preparation for a major action."

"Ah, well, we saw them travel into the belt. That's odd, but not definitive."

Struggling mightily to regain the initiative, she said, "My data analysis of your recent message translations is disturbing. I wish to relay a more generic view of the information to Fleet Headquarters," exposing her veiled objective.

"I disagree," said Gallant testing her resolve.

His comment was met with a cold reception.

She demanded, "Disagree? Why?" It was as if she stood on a precipice deciding where to step.

"We must protect our ability to spy on the Titans unobserved." Gallant paused before adding, "They have been intercepting and reading our communication for decades that's why we encrypt our secret messages. They don't bother with encryption because they believe we can't understand their communications. We must safeguard this fact until we have definitive information that will dramatically change the war, otherwise, once they realize we can read their messages they will begin encrypting everything, and our taps will be useless."

She said with emphasis, "But these messages may show a potential gathering point for a major operation, some general comments would be appreciated."

"We have not uncovered the details of this strategic military operation," he said. He would have liked to temporize, but it was already too late for such half measures. "We must wait until we get more specific data by spying on the Saturn headquarters."

Her sour face revealed her contrast opinion.

"Besides," he added, "we've learned a great deal about their society and philosophy."

"Really? You think we've achieved a significant understanding about the motivations of these creatures?" her tone was suspicious and cautious. She was distracted from her original train of thought and sounded like her sense of the situation was uncertain.

"Possibly," he gestured with a nod.

"I am uncertain how you were interpreting the meaning of certain words and phrases that lead you to these conclusions."

Enthusiasm appeared on Gallant's face as he said, "The autistic nature of the Titans makes their social skills limited. Understanding these limitations give us an opportunity to pursue political options—to consider the possibility of negotiating a settlement with this enemy."

She didn't respond. Her stunned look said more than words ever could. Finally, she said, "I can't help but feel you're exceeding your authority by speculating on this matter."

Gallant could tell he would get no further on this point with her, so he switched subjects. "There are several other points that you may also find troubling."

"Please go on. I can hardly wait to hear."

Gallant did not answer immediately but marshaled his thoughts in preparation for what he assumed would be a prolonged and difficult discussion. He reordered his ideas to meet the belligerent mood McCall displayed.

"It's an important matter," he said, "You told me in our previous discussions that the capacity to radically outperform the best human minds is called super-intelligence and that you were responsible for exploring this concept under the code name ENIGMA."

"Go on."

"There were several possibilities you were examining as emerging super-intelligence—natural mutation, genetic engineering, AI, and now savants."

She nodded and said, "As far as I can discern, emergence intelligence can represents a threat."

Gallant said, "You've considered AI and savants as mortal enemies in the past. You've never once explored the possibility of cohabitation with these life forms."

That was for her, a startling suggestion. A dark shadow fell across her face.

"Super-intelligence would vastly outperform human brains in creativity, social skills, and wisdom. Unleashing it may be humanity's legacy since once it is achieved, super-intelligence could self-improve and surpass itself."

"We started the twenty-first century with humans adding significant cognitive and physical enhancements through genetics, but there was a dramatic drop in beneficial mutations among genetically altered population. That's one reason you attracted such consternation."

Gallant frowned. He swallowed the realization that it was possible he would never be able to overcome that prejudice.

"Damn! Is that still a dilemma for you? Natural versus genetics?"

She said, "The ability of early super-intelligence to create greater abilities, and then produce next generation super-intelligence, means we must monitor burgeoning breakout types—like you. The onset of a more powerful intelligence could be swift and unstoppable. We have no understanding of the ethics or motivations of such beings. The question is: Do we aid the emergence or hinder it? We don't know."

It was an appalling thought for Gallant.

She said, "Collective super-intelligence is a system composed of a large number of small intellects such that the system's overall performance vastly outstrips current systems. That's our worry over the Titans."

"It's such a great concern that you won't even entertain the possibility of negotiating with them?"

McCall furrowed her brows before replying, "You are outside the parameters of your authority and your orders."

"Perhaps, but speaking of orders, your orders were not signed by Collingsworth. The high command sent you. With some prodding from Neumann, I'll bet, to spy on me even while I spy on the Titans. Was that with a consideration to gather court martial material against me?"

McCall stood and frowned again as she said, "He has nothing but the best interests of our people."

It was natural for her to argue such a point since it was to her own advantage.

"Is that how you're justifying spying on me? That's your cover story?" It pained him to hear his own words. He restrained himself from saying more that would further inflame the situation.

Her reaction surprised him.

"My orders are to evaluate the Titan information you collect. But, yes, I was also told to watch you and report on your performance. That was merely to understand the capabilities of a Natural, not to undermine you."

He failed to see anything incongruous in her words.

"I'm not here to play at genetic prejudices," she said. The furious look she projected at him, hit him as hard as an actual slap.

He rose and shifted his weight self-consciously from one foot to the other while remaining quiet.

She stared at him, but stifled any regrets about what she had said. After standing face to face with him for several moments, she settled back into her chair.

Gallant felt a silent rage against the uncontrolled fools who imperiled his mission for the sake of their own biases and self-interest.

While he was curious about her thinking process in pursuing this form of interaction, he wondered if this was a test of his character, or something deeper in her evaluation of his abilities.

He watched as her expression changed and she took a different tack. She said, "When people meet me, they see a pretty face and attractive figure. They never try to look past my appearance to learn about my abilities and character."

She waited to see if Gallant would object to that characterization. When he didn't, she continued, "I've learned to use my physical assets to become an SAI interrogation officer."

She complained peevishly. "I wish that weren't the case."

Her comments surprised Gallant.

She leaned forward as she said with relish, "And I'm good at it. I have a career that I have worked hard to develop. Yes I'm watching you, but you have my word that I will not subvert you or your command."

Gallant recalled her careful handling of him and the tact she had employed to garner knowledge of his personal feelings. He remained silent, but he was swayed by her argument.

Struggling mightily to regain her detached composure, she said, "Despite our personal difference, my data analysis of your recent message translations remains disturbing. It is now more evident that we should go directly to Saturn."

"I will consider your recommendation," he said rising to leave.

"By the way, Gallant," she said, causing him to halt beside the door, "we should talk once we learn more about the Titan's true intentions."

Gallant stared at her for a moment,

I wish I could discover your true intensions.

21

MINE FIELD

The captain of the *Warrior* was once more pacing along the limited space at the back of the bridge—as if he would discover something new each time he turned around, but he pretty much reached the same conclusion over and over again. The movement of the Titan armada into the asteroid belt was disturbing. After several bugging excursions to the moons orbiting Jupiter, they had gleaned a great deal of information and formed some important conjectures, but they still had no hard evidence about enemy fleet operations.

They could continue to operate around Jupiter and hope to find important information, or move to Saturn's strategic bases where it was more likely they could discover military secrets. It was Roberts' suggestion that they leave the recording devices in place and depart for Saturn immediately, leaving small nuclear mines with delayed fuses planted in strategic locations, such as high-traffic shipping lanes, so they wouldn't activate until the *Warrior* was well on her way to Saturn.

Gallant was curious to see what the enemy would do once the mines started to explode. How would they assess the danger? Would they guess the UP had stealth technology? Or would they assume the mines were the product of a minimum profile unmanned drone operation? Would they react aggressively and redirect all shipping or passively accept the losses? He made no attempt to enunciate any doubts that crossed his mind or how he would discuss the task in his reports.

The time was short for him to reach a decision. Mars needed fleet operations intelligence, but so far his reports lacked any hint of coordinated enemy fleet movements. This could all be quickly reversed with one significant message intercept, but the progress to date was not encouraging. Gallant sought order and discipline, but he was constantly faced with uncertainty instead. It was a horrible nuisance to deal with makeshift situations on a continuous basis. There was nothing intrinsically wrong in Roberts's suggestion, yet the burden fell on Gallant to make it happen.

The chatter on the bridge interrupted his thoughts and focused his attention back on the ship around him. For a moment he stood perplexed. Then he turned to his navigation team and asked them to check the ship's position. It was a full five minutes before he spoke again. He cursed the circumstances that had put him in this position.

Later that afternoon, Gallant held officers' call in the wardroom, but before he entered, he spent a minute fussing over his unsightly uniform. He didn't like setting such a bad example, but he had grown lazy about sleeping in his uniform. Once he entered, he took his place at the head of the wardroom table.

"The latest CIC assessment is that we've extracted operational information about Titan ships and facilities in the Jupiter system," Gallant explained, "and we have transmitted a complete report to Fleet Command, including Commander McCall's analysis. Unfortunately, though we've seen the armada in motion, we've uncovered no operational details about a major fleet attack."

"We've conducted over a dozen bugging operations here," said Roberts. "CIC agrees with my suggestion that it's time we close our Jupiter ops and move on to Saturn."

"We shouldn't be leaving until we've mined the Titan facilities," Clay said. "Let's get our priorities right. We need to do as much damage as we can." He then looked searchingly at Gallant.

Gallant probed the faces of his officers, trying to gauge their dispositions. Roberts displayed mental toughness and Walker was smart and eager, but both men lacked significant combat experience. There was raw tension in Clay as if he was a kettle on slow boil, impatient to strike the enemy. While morale was good throughout the ship, the crew was also anxious to move on to the next part of their mission.

"What's the status of weapon readiness?" Gallant asked.

"Sir, all mines are ready for deployment," said Clay. "My team is charging the battery and it will be at full capacity in an hour."

Gallant nodded. "Walker, what's the status of the ship's engines?"

The ship's engineer reported, "The sublight reactors are functioning nominally, thanks in large part to the efforts of Chief Howard to meet our maintenance requirements."

"Very well," said Gallant, coming to a decision. "We'll begin seeding mines today."

"Great," said Clay showing a smile for the first time.

A chorus of agreement followed from the other officers.

"Are there any other questions?" asked Gallant.

The officers remained quiet shaking their heads.

"Very well, gentlemen. Prepare your departments."

"I've been looking for some payback," said Clay showing his eagerness.

That afternoon the *Warrior* reached a position to carry out the mining operation. The captain was on the bridge, ready to go. He spared no one, including himself, driving as hard as he could to ensure the operation went off without incident. Since they were leaving the Jupiter area, it was no longer necessary to minimize attention to their operations. Having collected as much intelligence as he could around Jupiter, Gallant set about completing this sabotage before proceeding to Saturn. He decided to plant the mine field close to the Titan base and the high-traffic shipping lanes.

One of the problems of planting a mine field under the enemy's nose was that they would remove the mines if they became exposed. Another problem was that they might not detonate if poorly planted. The detections and detonation algorithm set into the mines had to be calibrated precisely for the area in which they were to be placed.

The *Warrior* moved into the traffic lane under stealth mode. It moved toward a picket ship and began the process of laying small AI-controlled mines. The men watched warily as the patrolling destroyers passed them on either beam without noticing the *Warrior* or the newly discharged mines.

The mines were set to activate in twenty-four hours, which would give the *Warrior* time to get far away. Gallant imagined the enemy would increase security once the explosions started. The civilian population might become alarmed as well, but that would be good.

There was always the temptation to linger to observe the first victim. That was always a mistake because once the area would become flooded with enemy military ships getting away undetected would become all but impossible.

Gallant thought,

It's time to move to Saturn and learn why the armada is moving.

22

BETWEEN PLANETS

Gallant tugged at his collar, letting perspiration trickle down his neck. His cabin was like an oven despite the herculean efforts of the ship's one remaining air conditioner to remove the residual heat coming from the many machines working within the *Warrior*.

He asked with resignation, "How much longer?"

With sweat dripping off his chin, Roberts replied, "Another hour, maybe two at the outside, sir." He wiped his streaming face with his sleeve, but in a minute it was wet again. The room continued to get stuffier and hotter.

The air conditioning system's maintenance should have been completed already, but a careless mistake by one of the men in engineering had damaged an essential piece of equipment and delayed matters. The ship's heat burden was now much worse than they had originally envisioned when Chief Howard had first proposed the procedure.

Roberts read Gallant's questioning face and said, "I've already double checked, sir. We've shutdown everything that we reasonably can." He shrugged: "Engines make heat."

Gallant said, "OK. OK. Let's try to forget the temperature. We still have ten days before we reach Saturn. We're behind in our maintenance upkeep and calibration tests, but I want you to choose projects more carefully, in order to avoid further delays."

"Yes, sir."

"I expect you to prioritize the work so that stealth technology gets priority."

"Yes, sir," said Roberts. "While I'm here, do you still wish to review personnel records?"

Gallant nodded and turned his eyes to the tablet detailing personnel records. They started by checking beneficiary and next of kin information. They discussed their performance and set up meetings with individuals who could use guidance.

"Another thing I'd like to discuss, skipper, is the personnel lessons we've learned from our Jupiter operations."

'Such as?"

"Such as, men staying on watch for six hours continuously at one station, sir. I'd like the bridge crew to rotate between stations during their six hour cycle. It will help with cross-training and keep them alert."

"I like that."

They set up a new rotation for the watch schedule to give the men some fresh experience.

"What else?"

Roberts said, "There is a newly qualified engine room PO. I knew I had seen him before, but couldn't place him. It turns out he was one of the weapons techs who trained me when I was a midshipman. He remembers me and my habit of overshooting the target. He razzed me back then and now he's apprehensive that I wouldn't be so forgiving. We had a good laugh. Anyway, I want to add him to the engineering rotation, and there are two more men close to finishing weapons qualifications."

"Very well."

"Also, sir, I think we need to get on the men about physical fitness. I've notice a few waistlines growing as well as a few tails dragging. Exercise would do them good."

"You're kidding?" asked Gallant. "How can they put on weight while living on a diet of synthetic rations?"

"Well, sir, I suspect there is a stash of special treats that was hidden away by a few individuals. They're enjoying them while they can. If you keep your eye open you can catch them nibbling away in the dark corners of the operations compartment."

"I wouldn't be surprised."

"If there's a will there's a way," chuckled Roberts with a grin.

Before long they set up a physical activity schedule and hoped the crew would begin stretching their muscles accordingly. The four-man gym, over the reactor compartment, would be kept busy with calisthenics and weights exercises. Oddly, racquetball was expected to become a favorite in the confined box-like space.

The average age of the crew was twenty-one with only a few senior chiefs, like Howard, tipping the scale a bit. Men like Howard were respected for their experience and expertise. It was the senior ranks that provided the continuity and steadfastness for the crew. But the age of the crew also had a lot to do with their chosen activities.

Gallant asked, "What do you think of our crew's overall performance?"

Roberts replied, "Well, skipper, my family is from Earth, but many on board were brought here from a variety of towns, drawn from the planets and colonies throughout the Solar System. The families of the crew reflect all walks of life and education. Everyone was a volunteer with a strong sense of pride and a respect for authority. As a result, these men possess a special value system."

"I would agree."

Roberts continued, "They may prefer to be home romancing their sweethearts, but they've accepted that they are caught up in this war. They know serving is more than just a job. While many of them have never served together, I believe they are, for the most part, idealists seeking a sense of 'family' within an elite outfit."

"Well," Gallant said, "the *Warrior* can provide that sense of an elite unit, but it's up to us to train and harden these men. In the end, they will develop a bond from shared experiences and learn to trust the shipmate next to them."

Roberts nodded with the satisfaction of having reached an understanding with his captain.

Together they scheduled exercises for stealth operations and target practice for the weapons batteries.

Gallant reviewed the Jupiter message data they had stolen from the aliens in the hope that there was some gem of information that he had missed earlier. In addition, he took time away from his study of Titan communications to train Gabriel on Wasp maneuvers and operations.

In the meantime, the crew's transition from conducting dangerous operations to routine travel was surprisingly quick. The first few days were filled with the housework of cleaning bodies, uniforms, and personal spaces. Then they found time for a good deal of relaxation from games, movies, and sleep.

Two days later, Gallant commented to Roberts, "I've noticed Gabriel was late for several training sessions recently and he has also fallen behind in his qualification program. He was supposed to take the AI administered exams on the schedule it laid out in order to qualify as a duty officer on the ship."

"I think the problem is the competition he's had along with several members of the crew," said Roberts.

"Competition?"

"A simulation game tournament. It turns out that he's a wiz at it and he's taking on all comers. You know the fast reflexes of youth versus the hard experience of veterans."

Gamers often enjoyed competing aboard ships, and many put their money where their mouths were when tournaments were involved. Flying and shooting simulations enjoyed special attention. The Warrior's techs had a long history of local tournaments for points, or just plain bragging rights, but now more gamers were battling head to head on some ships for prize money. Gabriel was considered an expert with AI cyber games. He competed in several formats, but the most common was single or double elimination. The popularity of fighting games included first-person shooters. Some games included a wide variety of military battles. These genres maintained a devoted fan base within the fleet. In addition to allowing players to participate in a given game, there were observing features for spectators. This offered others a chance to watch the game unfold from the competitors' point of view. It included a highly modified interface for the spectators to access information even the players didn't have.

"Gambling?" Gallant asked, speculatively.

"Oh, no, sir," said Roberts, and then backtracking, "Well, I don't think so, at least nothing beyond a few tokens." Then shaking his head, "No, I doubt there is anything beyond that."

Gallant looked at Roberts, doubtfully.

"I'll look into it, sir," said Roberts.

Gallant couldn't be sure, but he definitely didn't like secret activities. He said, "OK. If it's really harmless, I don't wish to interfere. However, be on guard and make sure it remains harmless."

Was there, or was there not, something more involved?

23

SATURN

Ten days after leaving Jupiter, the Warrior approached Saturn. Although only one-eighth of Earth's density, the pale yellow gas giant was nearly one hundred times larger and surrounded by 150 moons. Just over 1.2 million kilometers from the planet was its largest moon, Titan. The ice moon had its own methane-rich atmosphere and when the sun's ultraviolet radiation struck the atmosphere, it rained liquid methane. The aliens' origin was believed to be a planet of the red dwarf Gliese-581, located 20.5 light years away, but because the Titan moon served as the aliens' main population center in the Solar System, the United Planets had nicknamed the aliens "Titans."

Rhea, the second largest moon, also had a tenuous atmosphere. The moons Pandora and Prometheus acted as gravitational shepherds to confine the planetary rings and prevent spreading while the moons Pan and Atlas caused waves within those rings.

The rings themselves appeared like grooves in a vinyl record. The most prominent rings were thick, composed of ice and impurities, with particle sizes ranging from dust to ten meters. There were also faint rings further out from Saturn with wide gaps between them.

The *Warrior* began collecting information about the strength of the Titan fleet in the area and the development of its colonization. The bridge crew was aghast at the incredible infrastructure the aliens had developed on so many of the moons. It was going to be a challenge to operate in such a heavily populated and trafficked environment, but the stealth and cloaking technology allowed the *Warrior* to penetrate deep into the alien territory unobserved.

The Titans had built their main military headquarters on Pandora. It had a layered defense with satellites, minefields, and overlapping fields of fire from fortresses with scores of missile launchers guarding the approaches. The obstructing strong points were a hazard to navigate.

The CIC tech reported, "The Titan industry and population infrastructure, as well as military strength show a number of energy emission sites, indicating communities and industries in hundreds of locations. Our population estimate is between ten to fifty million for Saturn's moons. These estimates don't correlate with a long term civilization on Saturn, unless there are billions more underground. But they would need a huge underground industry, as well. My guess would be they have inhabited Saturn's moons for less than a century."

The *Warrior* stayed behind the Titan ships as she moved through rings. This allows them to disguise their wake while Gallant focused his attention on surveying the region to find a location for their new support base.

They set up a relay communication station, designated Base Kepler, on a remote moon away from most of the alien's bases. It provided secure shelter for recharging the stealth batteries. It was designed similar to their base at Jupiter.

※

When she arrived at Jupiter, the *Warrior* had been a novice. Now, she was a veteran. Ten days of hard work as they journeyed from Jupiter had improved their training. Constant drills and the repeated instructions were applied with tempered discipline and good humor. It had made a positive impact on the crew.

While Gallant planned the deployment of tapping devices and explosives for this planetary system, he found Clay constantly prodding him to do more.

One day, Gallant poked his head into the crew's mess to see how they were reacting to the new activities. The mess hall was fairly crowded having just completed lunch service. The crew was relaxing by playing games and telling tales. Music played softly in the background and several video games were underway on one of the rear tables. There was a wide disparity in the crew's dress. Some were in uniform while others wore special gear for engineering room repairs, or weapons tube maintenance that required exterior protection. One weapon tech was wearing fire-retardant dungarees. The noise level was high—giving the impression of a controlled madhouse.

"Good day," Gallant said loudly over the racket.

The conversations stopped as they turned toward him. Several crew members started to rise, but he said, "At ease."

A moment later, he asked, "Can I join you for a few minutes?"

There was a spattering of "Yes, sirs," while they made room for him at one of the center tables.

Muffled noises were heard as food plates were shoved aside.

Gallant was glad to see lots of interested faces.

"How are things going with you?" He asked a nearby petty officer.

"It's different, sir. Lot's different from my last ship. We mostly patrolled against raiders near Mars. I never expected any of this."

The chatter in the mess grew appreciably.

Gallant sat down and connected a tablet to the console screen at the head of the compartment.

"This is Saturn," he said, as the screen came alive with the huge image. "And this is our preliminary assessment of the layout of the enemy installations."

"Wow," was the general reaction.

He said, "The *Warrior* is now ready to flex her muscles." This caused a lot of chatter.

A heavy set man with sleepy eyes leaned forward to get a better view. He asked, "Where are we going to be operating, sir?"

Gallant recalled talking with this engineering petty officer several times before. He responded, "Good question, Gonzales. See that mid-sized moon close to Saturn? It's called Pandora and is the military headquarters of the entire operation. We're going to be conducting tapping and bugging operations on several of the moons and bases in this planet's system, but Pandora is the prize jewel. It is also the hardest nut to crack because it is located in the densest part of the rings."

"Are we supposed to reconnoiter that base, sir?" asked a dark complexioned young man.

Gallant recognized him as a CIC tech. "Yes, Jackson, that and more."

One crewman with a half-finished synthetic food bar in his hand commented, "There are a lot of aliens here."

"Would you guys like to know what's here?" asked Gallant.

"Sure would, sir." The enthusiasm caught on. The crew was beaming with excitement.

"May I ask a question, sir?"

"Sure," said Gallant.

"What's going on?"

"What are you referring to?" said Gallant.

"I mean, we go in we drop some stuff, we come out, but we don't shoot anybody. Why not?"

"Oh, well, as you may notice we're pretty well out numbered here," said Gallant. "If any shooting starts, we might not do so well."

That produced a chuckle.

"Yeah, but we have the cloak for protection."

"That's true, but to shoot we have to drop the cloak, and even so, they would know where the shooting is coming from the minute we shot. No, ours is a game of stealth."

Gallant said "I want you to know, I will take every reasonable precaution, but our job is to be aggressive and penetrate deep into the enemy's most highly guarded places. We have great new technology to keep us hidden, but we've already found that it's not infallible. We're going on this mission with our eyes open. We will take advantage of everything that helps us obtain intelligence on the aliens' intentions and movements. We're going to steal every piece of data that's not bolted down."

The sincere words made a deep impression on them.

He allowed them to discuss things openly amongst themselves which resulted in a great deal of second guessing of tactics and strategy, but by far the favorite topic was when they would get back home.

"By the way, I'm forming a trouble squad for a dangerous mission. Let me know if there are any takers."

"Huh, sir. What's the deal? What have you got in mind?"

"You'll see."

As he was leaving, he heard whispers, "The old man's hunting for bear."

Gallant's ears perked up . . . *Old man?*

24

TRAILING

Saturn's rings were less dense in the vicinity of the moon, Titan, but Gallant approached it with caution nonetheless. He had completed a number of sorties through enemy territory already and it should've been old stuff, by now, but, of course, it wasn't. Each excursion was fraught with its own unique sets of dangers. If he were looking for ease and safety, he would have stayed several hundred million kilometers away.

After a few swift observations, he selected his target. "That cargo ship has a huge mass and a broad beam. It's moving slowly and it has a wide turning radius. It appears to be heading in the right direction, so I think it'll create a significant enough turbulence to hide our wake if we follow close behind it. We'll sneak up on her stern and follow her through the rings. Once we're past the satellites, and sensor arrays, we should be close enough to the moon to conduct our operation."

"Set course and speed to follow close behind the cargo ship," ordered Gallant.

"Aye aye, sir," said Lieutenant Clay, who was the current Officer of the Deck.

CIC was looking over the cargo ship carefully and logging its characteristics.

"Bridge, CIC; We designate this target as Kilo-one."

"Very well," said the OOD. "CIC, bridge; Keep a sharp watch for any rapid maneuvers by the target. Also, keep a careful watch on our wake and inform me, immediately, if any other ships show an interest in it."

"Aye aye, sir," responded CIC.

Gallant entered CIC and examined the complicated traffic pattern. He had the navigator plot a course through the rings—past the satellites and orbiting fortifications. He hoped he could use Kilo-one to get them most of the way there. If not, he would have to find another ship to trail. The CIC analysts were diligently plotting the tracks of every ship along their general direction.

The *Warrior* was a fine ship, but Gallant had noticed a slight imperfection in her handling at slower speeds.

He spoke through the public address system, "Shipmates, today we are going to investigate the enemy's base on Titan. For us, there are now two types of spacecraft; the *Warrior* and . . . targets," he paused to allow what he expected would be a few chortles.

He continued, "We can expect trailing operations to be trickier than those we experienced around Jupiter because of the tremendous number of sensors and ships in the area, as well as the denser rings of Saturn. These rings will expose our turbulence wake despite our stealth technology. We're going to whip the turbulence problem by trailing close behind enemy shipping and letting their wakes disguise ours. This will become the ultimate test of our stealth capabilities. It will also test our ship handling skills to travel at high speeds close to enemy ships."

He paused again and then said, "We'll take the *Warrior* close to the dark side of this moon and launch the Wasp carrying Mr. Gabriel and myself. We'll land on the moon and perform an EVA to plant a bug at the alien's communication junction manifold. But we'll be back aboard before anyone is the wiser."

There was an audible "Aaaahhh," from the crew, no doubt from their collective hearts beating faster.

Gallant murmured, "This should prove to be a memorable mission."

He turned and nodded to the OOD. He said, "Proceed."

Clay set the *Warrior's* course to follow Kilo-one.

Clay told the bridge crew, "We'll creep up on him. Stay alert."

CIC maintained a track on the target and plotted all the nearby shipping to ensure none passed close enough to interfere with the *Warrior*.

Of course, there was no guarantee of success, even if they didn't make a mistake. The fortunes of war were such, that any one of a million random events could thwart them.

"Anything new on radar?"

CIC responded, "No, sir."

Gallant said, "We're committed to this course of action. Let's prove we can trail this ship as close as necessary."

As they reached position directly behind the target they adjusted speed to close to within a distance that gave them a ten second window to react if the target abruptly changed speed or course.

As they trailed Kilo-one their turbulence merged with that of the cargo ship.

They passed close to a second sensor array without detection.

Kilo-one seemed indifferent to the large rocks it was passing, as though it knew them all, intimately. For the *Warrior*, however, they presented a serious navigational hazard.

Kilo-one moved through the faint rings that were common at this distance from Saturn and passed between a pair of 1 km rocks that were traveling at nearly the same speed as each other. It was the 'nearly' that presented a problem because as the *Warrior* made its approach to pass, the rocks moved closer together.

Gallant looked at the CIC analyst and said, "Well?"

After a quick calculation, he responded, "We're OK, sir."

The *Warrior* followed its target and the process kept the bridge crew on edge.

"Bridge, Kilo-one is executing a turn to starboard," bellowed a CIC analyst.

The OOD order, "Helm, all stop," halted the engine drive and let the ship's momentum carry them forward.

"Aye aye, sir."

A short distance ahead of the *Warrior*, her contact completed her turn. As the target straightened out her course again, the OOD ordered, "Helm, ahead one third, come right to new heading 120, mark two."

The course change brought the *Warrior* back into position behind the contact.

Countering the target's maneuver was not just tricky—it was dangerous. Given the proximity of the two ships, a collision was possible. In addition, the maneuver would also leave a bewildering wake turbulence that might stir up a curious patrol ship, possibly revealing the *Warrior*.

As they trailed the contact, the OOD was careful to maintain a constant distance.

"Distance to target is now standard length. We're getting indications that she has settled on her course and speed. The contact is moving in a routine manner without a suggestion of detecting us."

"Well done," Gallant said, "We completed the maneuver and they don't have a clue we even exist."

Kilo-one increased speed at one point for a short distance and then slowed dramatically as it approached its parking orbit. The *Warrior* slowed and moved away, careful not to stir up too significant a wake.

"We have company," said Clay, as another vessel passed close, producing some apprehension.

"How many contacts do we have within one million km?" asked Gallant.

"There are twenty-seven contacts within that radius, but fourteen are underway," reported CIC.

"What's the bearing to the closest?"

"Bearing 090, mark two."

Gallant studied the chart and ordered the *Warrior* to follow behind the new target which was designated Kilo-two.

After trailing the ship for several minutes, the *Warrior* found the repetitive operations of the target to be of considerable advantage. They attempted to collect individual ship characteristics and signatures for their database with the belief they might follow the same ships multiple times.

The tactical situation was becoming clear. After surveying the best landing position for the Wasp, the *Warrior* parked in a stationary orbit.

"What is the disposition of the military patrol ships in this region?" asked Gallant.

The OOD said, "Sir, there are a half dozen warship that have begun to move and rendezvous over the north polar coordinates of the moon." He showed a plot of two views superimposed to make clear which ships were moving.

"Could we have spooked them?"

"Not likely, sir."

After several more minutes, that assessment proved correct. The warships left the area on an unknown mission.

"That was good training for us. We'll be doing a lot of trailing and analysis in the future."

With the *Warrior* parked in orbit over Titan under stealth mode. Gallant got dressed in his pressure suit for the Wasp mission.

"Send Gabriel to the flight deck. I'll let you know when we're ready for launch."

"Yes, sir."

Gabriel made his way to the hangar bay and together they climbed in the ship and prepared for launch. Gallant strapped into the command chair and pulled the neural interface over his head. He connected to the AI flight controls and started the engines.

Gabriel gave him a thumbs-up, eager to embrace the adventure.

"Bridge, Wasp; we're ready for launch," said Gallant.

The OOD said, "Wasp, bridge; launch vehicle."

The acceleration thrust the two passengers against their seats as the craft left the *Warrior*.

"Activate stealth mode," ordered Gallant.

"Aye aye, sir," said Gabriel, as he pulled on his neural interface and formed a mental image of the stealth controls while Gallant piloted the craft.

Soon the tiny vehicle approached the moon in stealth mode.

"Give me a detailed operational status."

"Yes, sir. I'll get a fix now, sir."

Gabriel appeared nervous. However, he was making every effort to be alert and do his job.

When the Wasp landed on Titan, it came to rest on the surface at the edge of a plateau. Its two occupants prepared for an EVA. Gallant ambled to the access hatch on the side of the ship. They gathered the bugging device and exited the ship. Bouncing along the surface, they made their way toward their objective, a communication distribution station.

The sun hit a nearby boulder which cast a long shadow across their path. Gallant looked up into space searching to see if they had any unwanted company.

Nothing there; good.

When they reached the communication junction box, they opened the hatch and chose the cable to attach the bug to. There were no guards in the vicinity of the junction box. The problem of bugging the aliens on this moon was less formidable than he had thought.

They worked for the better part of an hour before Gallant was satisfied. He listened to several transmissions to be sure the device was operating properly and transcribed the first message to see if it made sense. The message said, in effect, that a certain military unit was to move. He guessed it was a routine operation.

Gallant realized that even collecting important data was not going to do any good, unless he got better at understanding the content of the messages. The next message appeared to be a general message addressing the public announcing a victory in battle and claiming to having defeated a large force of humans in the asteroid belt. There were no precise figures or details of the combat. He surmised it was a propaganda notice to keep their civilian population pacified.

They left the bugging device in place to record messages while they were gone and then they made their way back to the Wasp. They were about half way there when they noticed a shuttle craft pass overhead, but it passed without incident.

They felt lucky to avoid threats, both real and imagined. When they emerged from the outcropping of rocks they got aboard the Wasp and lifted off.

After rendezvousing with the *Warrior*, they left the moon's orbit.

"Find a suitable ship for us to trail in order to exit the area," Gallant ordered.

25

GABRIEL

Gallant held the stylus loosely in his right hand and let it flow gently over the drawing tablet's surface, tracing a thin curved line along the contour of the facial image. The faint stroke added to an existing collection of marks, composing the striking features of a beautiful woman. He held his breath and examined the sketch with a critical eye, observing all of its multifaceted flaws, as well as its inadequacy to capture the true underlying beauty of his model.

In the background, an aria from a classic opera was playing that suited his mood. This artistic outpouring provided Gallant with a tranquil respite after weeks of tension-filled espionage operations and he had come to cherish these diversions for a few hours each week.

An unwelcome knock on his cabin door interrupted his serenity. He put the drawing down on his desk and begrudgingly said, "Enter."

The door opened a crack and Midshipman Gabriel peeked inside, aware that he was trespassing into sacred territory.

"I'm sorry to disturb your rest period, sir," said a deferential, but unrepentant voice.

"Never mind," said Gallant. He turned the music down and asked, "What do you need?"

Gabriel entered the cabin and stood at attention. He spoke excitedly, "You said I should see you as soon as I passed my pilot qualification exams. Chief Howard has signed off on my last AI administrated exam." He held a tablet in his outstretched hand for Gallant's inspection.

"At ease," said Gallant, taking the tablet. He looked down at the long list of qualification check-offs that the midshipman had completed. The last one had been signed by Chief Howard a mere ten minutes earlier. He then cast a lingering look at Gabriel who squirmed under his commanding officer's scrutiny.

Finally, Gallant said, "Congratulations. You're ready to solo in the Wasp. I'll make arrangements for your qualifying flight the next time we recharge batteries at Base Kepler."

Beaming, Gabriel said, "Thank you, sir." However, lost in the excitement of the moment, he remained firmly rooted where he was standing.

The musical recording chose that moment to reach a loud crescendo. The expressive melody caught Gabriel's attention, and, in a distracted voice, he remarked, "I've never heard music like that before."

He was so entranced, that he left out the obligatory, 'sir,' which Gallant forgivingly let pass.

"It's a classical opera. It stimulates my imagination while I sketch," said Gallant, longing to return to his leisure activity, yet patient enough to let the young man express himself.

"It's beautiful, sir," said Gabriel with admiration. He had entered the private world of his commanding officer and was exposing a touch of hero worship.

"It's one of my favorite pieces," said Gallant. He listened as the music rose and the sweet soprano voice extended a lingering note's emotional impact.

"What language is that, sir?"

"Italian."

"Do you mind if I ask, what's she saying, sir?" the freckled face was eager to drink in the experience.

"She's singing about an officer whose ship travels to a foreign land where he falls in love with a native girl—it ends in tragedy, I'm afraid," said Gallant, letting his mind wander over the majesty of the more expansive version of the tale he reviewed in his mind.

"It's mesmerizing, sir. I love it." Turning his attention to Gallant's sketch, Gabriel, once more, commented impulsively, "She's lovely."

Gallant sighed,

This young man is so free in expressing his feelings.

"Is she someone special, sir?"

"Yes. Her name is Alaina. Unfortunately, she is very far away." He paused, deciding he didn't want to discuss his personal relationships, so he turned the question around, "Do you have someone back home?

"Yes, sir. My hometown sweetheart, Jennifer. I've loved her from the moment we met." He added unabashed. "I'll marry her someday."

"Someday?"

"Well, yes, sir. After this deployment, I'll be promoted, and I hope I'll be stationed back on Mars. You'll see, everything will work out perfectly."

Gallant smiled wistfully, wondering if Jennifer would still be waiting.

"Will you marry Alaina, sir?" asked the midshipman shamelessly.

Gallant paused and then gave a half-hearted shrug to express his actual uncertainty.

"Do you mind if I give you some advice, sir? Love is fleeting—you should embrace it while you can—you'd never forgive yourself if you let it get away," said Gabriel with all the smug astuteness his seventeen years permitted.

Stunned by the presumption of the youth, Gallant took a moment before ultimately deciding there was wisdom in his words.

26

PANDORA

Gallant slept badly that night and woke in a positively cross mood. Still feeling the aftereffects of his last mission—it took several minutes before he shook off a variety of aches and pains. His head was filled with disturbing visions of strange people. He gave his mind a chance to evaluate the lingering qualms of his dreams. As he remained sitting in bed—waiting for his black mood to fall away—his scowl morphed into a neutral acceptance of the day. By the time he made his way to the bridge, he was ready for the daunting day ahead.

The *Warrior*'s exploits had become more and more exciting as they treaded closer and closer to danger. And with each successful operation, the crew's confidence grew. While confidence is generally good, it can also lead to carelessness. It was important to remember that the dangers they faced were real, ever present, and could materialize at a moment's notice, even if the crew was not noticing them as much.

From the priority messages Gallant had recently translated, he was beginning to piece together a Titan plan that involved the entire armada in a major attack. Such information needed to be validated and updated, driving him to take increased risk to acquire messages from higher military authorities.

The highest Titan authority was on Pandora at the main military headquarters. Gallant hoped to collect and decode communications from this facility to learn their most secret operations. By now the *Warrior* was an old hand at penetrating enemy positions and planting and collecting bugs, but he knew he had to be alert for this day's task because while Pandora was likely to have the most valuable intelligence, it was also likely to be the most dangerous mission for that very reason.

When Gallant came onto the bridge, Roberts frowned and said, "Sir, you've been driving yourself very hard the last few weeks. Don't you think we might relax the schedule for a day, or so, and give everyone a chance to rest?"

"I wish we had that luxury, but the recent messages all indicate that the aliens are getting ready for something big. We can't afford to take time off now. We're schedule to tackle Pandora today and that's what we'll do.

"This is the Titan's playground," Roberts pointed out, "They're likely to be touchy about visitors."

"They seem to be creatures of habit. We should be able to take advantage of their routine operations."

"We're going to have to follow a few ships on the way to our designated location."

"Check with CIC for what ships are appropriate."

The *Warrior* glided confidently through the rings at slow speed. The enemy sensor arrays sounded no alert.

The sensor tech reported, "Closest point of approach to array is 50 km."

"Bridge, CIC; contact bearing 233, mark one."

"Very well."

"Bridge, CIC; contact has zero bearing rate."

"Helm, increase your rudder to right full," said the OOD.

"Increase rudder to right full, helm, aye, sir."

"Skipper, what are we dealing with?""Someone was alert aboard the destroyer. The picket ship got a whiff of something, but couldn't tell what. Now they're heading in the *Warrior's* direction."

Gallant gave orders to switch to ultra-stealth mode putting out its lowest profile.

What he needed was some good luck. Everybody on board realized the risk they were taking. It was a nerve-racking business. There were a few ships they could trail. Gallant chose one and headed for it.

"Here she comes."

A cargo ship came close enough to the *Warrior* and she glided behind it unobserved. The sigh of relief was universally throughout the ship as their wake was safely disguised.

As Gallant looked at the view screen, he could see that the inner area was alive with activity. Ships traveled between the inner moons and satellites. At the outer edges where the *Warrior* was, there were picket ships interspersed with an early warning satellite system. The *Warrior's* trajectory would pass close to many listening posts.

One of the picket ships altered course slightly toward the *Warrior*.

Soon it was time for Gallant and Gabriel to go to the launch bay.

When the Warrior reached the set distance, Roberts said, "Wasp, bridge; launch vehicle."

The craft departed the *Warrior*.

"Activate stealth mode," ordered Gallant going through the routine operations, as he and Gabriel flew the Wasp close to Pandora. Pandora was an especially difficult moon to approach because it was located in one of the densest sectors of Saturn's rings.

Gallant said, "Take the flight controls, Gabriel."

Since Gabriel had successfully completed his sole flight qualifications in the Wasp, Gallant had given him more and more responsibility for operating the craft and the precocious young man was doing exceptionally well.

As the vehicle approached the moon, Gabriel controlled the flight path with great precision and they reached the point where he could land on the moon. They disembarked and began their EVA to the communication junction box.

The general area was guarded and they had to proceed with caution. There was a path cut into the rocks that led to the communication junction box. They began their work of collecting the secret messages the communication junction box offered.

"Wait!" Gallant whispered harshly.

There was a motion near the building. A guard was coming.

They hid and waited for the guard to pass.

He adjusted his oxygen flow rate when he found himself using more than usual. Eventually they finished their work and made their way back to the Wasp.

When they returned to the Wasp, they took off. The Wasp trailed behind Titan ships as they moved through the rings. A pair of picket ships lumbered across their course, bumbling along a trajectory intended to alert the system of intruders, yet having failed to detect them.

On their journey back to the *Warrior*, Gallant poked his nose further into the deployment of enemy ships. He was able to identify numerous cruisers and destroyers assembled in orbit. Maintaining a database of each ship that they could catalog was helpful in identifying the location where they reported and how they maneuvered.

They kept their attention on keeping track of the ring debris so that they could avoid leaving a wake or any signal that could be picked up by the Titan destroyers on picket duty.

EEERRRRR!

The siren went off on the Wasp.

"We have an overload in the engine," said Gallant.

Gabriel said, "I'm seeing harmonic vibration in the stealth containment field."

"Try to compensate and keep the system stable," said Gallant as he fought to do the same with the engine drive system.

Gabriel said, "I think our cloak is fluctuating. We may become visible!"

Gabriel worked hard to restore the cloak controls while Gallant adjusted the propulsion system.

The neural interface allowed each of the men to focus their mental energies on balancing the modulation and frequency of the field. Slowly they regained control and reestablish the harmonic balance. The cloak was fully restored and the engines returned to full power.

The scary moment disappeared as Gallant and Gabriel worked together.

A few minutes later they were back on course, operating normally.

Fortunately the enemy ships passed without siting them.

"We're slipping through, sir."

Moments later they relaxed for the first time in hours.

"Good job, Gabe," said Gallant using his nickname for the first time. It felt right.

Gabriel lit up enthusiastically, "Thank you, sir."

When they rendezvoused with *Warrior*, they docked.

"Let's get aboard the *Warrior*," said Gallant, glad the mission was over.

As Gallant got out of the Wasp, he ordered Chief Howard to check the Wasp to see what caused malfunction.

27

COLLECTING

Repeatedly, Gallant had to conduct missions in the Wasp to sneak back to the moons and collect recorded data, and then leave, without arousing the aliens' suspicion. The operations meant stealth incursions into highly trafficked and well-guarded bases. It called for cunning to collect the information, recalibrate the recorders, and get back to safety. Before each operation, he played every possible permutation in his mind as if he were playing chess. However, in this game, his opponents were genius autistic savants. They had unique AI networking abilities and their own interpretation of game theory. His brain had to account for their complex thought processes.

He wondered.

Can I really outthink them?

A tap at Gallant's cabin door brought a growl, "Come in."

It was Midshipman Gabriel.

"Mr. Clay sent me, sir. He says there are activities at the entrance to the base that you should look at if you have the time, sir."

"Very well. I'll come."

It was a peculiarity of some officers of the deck to send a runner, rather than to use the ships communication channels, to alert the captain of lower priority information. Gallant wasn't exactly sure why that had developed as a preference for certain types of reports—perhaps it kept down the level of stress.

As he entered the bridge, he looked at the forward portal and the AI consoles to see what had stirred the OOD's attention.

Clay said, "It's a general broadcast signal. The Titans are sending a signal to all the ships around Saturn. We've never seen this before, sir."

"What the devil are they doing?" asked Gallant.

"Maybe it's a transfer of supplies. A last minute activity?" suggested Clay.

Gallant spent a few more minutes speculating then he said, "Let CIC analyze this signal. I'm going back to my cabin."

In his cabin, he opened up the communications panel and looked once more at his orders specific to this type of operation.

He began to rise from his chair unconsciously pacing back and forth on the restricted deck, five steps forward, and five steps back.

Finally, Gallant stretched out on his cot, waiting for time to pass, hoping he could fall asleep, but sleep would not come. It was better to lie there and rest regardless of how fidgety he was.

A few hours later, Gallant got aboard the two-man craft. He ran his eyes up and down over the console panels reading the parameters. They were off on another collection mission.

With Gallant on a mission Lieutenant Clay had a chance to contemplate his situation. He sat in the command chair on the bridge of the *Warrior*. He touched the console screen and pulled up a vast array of virtual controls capable of monitoring and directing every aspect of the ship. Part of his brain concentrated on recovering the Wasp from her latest excursion on the Titan moon. He swiped a screen to display a three dimensional image of Pandora. The moon was as harsh as ever and posed a deadly threat. The methane atmosphere was volatile with periodical bursts of volcano activity.

A sentry destroyer turned toward the *Warrior*. Clay leaned forward, his hands tightly gripping the chair, his jaw jutted out, he said, "Helm, slow to one third. CIC find us a slow moving freighter we can trail."

"Aye, aye, sir," came the voice from CIC.

"Helm, set course 150, mark two," said Clay.

"Aye aye, sir." A moment later, "Sir, steady course on 150, mark two."

"Very Well."

Powerful and majestic, the *Warrior* passed high above the moon.

A few minutes later, CIC said, "The destroyer is maneuvering closer."

"Helm. Ahead two-thirds," ordered Clay.

"Aye, aye, sir."

Slowly the *Warrior* clawed her way out of orbit and toward safety, away from the moon. All eyes clung to the screen following their trajectory.

If Clay were asked to be specific about what irked him most about Gallant, he couldn't articulate it. He only knew Gallant had a unique mental faculty to interface with AI controls—far surpassing Clay's own talents. While he waited, he considered what it meant to lead men in battle. It wasn't merely to demonstrate ship handling skills, or marksmanship, or to be conversant with the petty and trifling requirements of ship's operations, or to be master of thousands of details—it was necessary to exhibit bold decisive initiative, moral as well as physical courage, and, ingenuity and quickness of thought. He was beginning to appreciate Gallant.

Clay was brought back to the present by a squawk from the computer console. The cat and mouse game with the enemy ship continued for nearly an hour. Clay's eyes were glued to the screen as it flickered before him and went blank.

Clay watched the screens around him as the minutes tick by. A bead of sweat formed on his forehead, threatening to roll down his genetically perfect face. He swiped it away.

The *Warrior* continued to wait.

After about ten minutes they made their approach to recover the Wasp. Once it was on board, Gallant came to the bridge.

"Evening, sir," said Lieutenant Clay.

"Evening," answered Gallant.

"There's considerable planet turbulence, sir."

"It shouldn't be a problem for us."

"No, sir, but it'll get worse before long, sir."

Gallant grunted.

Clay concluded, "It's an interesting phenomenon."

Later that evening, Roberts, Clay, and Gabriel joined Gallant in the wardroom for dinner. Gallant sat at the head of the table and as tradition demands played host to his officers. The Warrior was on its way to Base Kepler to transmit their latest report.

"I'm sure you gentlemen will forgive the meager fair of synthetics this evening. We still haven't repaired the main food synthesizer."

"This is better than syn-em, sir," said Gabriel.

"Syn-em?" asked Gallant vaguely.

"Yes, sir," said Gabriel, guilt faced.

Roberts said, "Syn-em is the nickname for the oldest bars of **syn**thetic food normally stored in **em**ergency ration packs in the escape pods. It can keep you alive if you had to abandon ship, but some say that after eating Syn-em for a while, you might wish that wasn't the case."

"I hope you haven't been breaking into the emergency packs," said Gallant.

"Oh no, sir. Not I. It's just that I've heard rumors, is all," said Gabriel.

"Mr. Roberts, please see that the emergency packages are fully stocked and post a notice that pilfering such supplies is frowned upon."

"Aye aye, sir."

"Did you ever eat syn-em on you other ships, sir?" asked Gabriel innocently.

In reply to such a direct question, Gallant was compelled to lie, "Of course not."

Roberts grinned.

"Let's return to our meal," said Gallant.

They finished the unappetizing food, reluctant to leave unsatisfied when they were interrupted by a siren . . .

EEEEERRRRRRRR!!!

The siren blared throughout the *Warrior*. Over the public address system, the engineering officer of the watch reported, "Radiation leak in the reactor compartment. Radiation leak in the reactor compartment."

Seconds later the speakers clamored, "Reactor emergency. Reactor emergency."

A ship is only as good as its crew and a single human error during nuclear power operations can jeopardize everyone on board. If any man lacks judgment, or initiative, the ship can be imperiled. It takes absolute determination to overcome serious accidents and no accident aboard ship is more serious than a reactor accident.

A reactor emergency required the swift shutdown of the nuclear fusion reactor. It is the ultimate safety action taken to prevent reactor core damage in crisis situations, such as over-power condition or an under-cooling condition. It involves the rapid insertion of substantial negative reactivity, usually by injection of control rods into the reactor fuel core. This diminished the nuclear fusion process, and substantially reduces power production. The action was initiated manually by the reactor operator when a fire started in the control rod panel.

Gallant bound from the wardroom to the bridge.

"Bridge, engineering; there has been a failure in the reactor control system and a minor leak has developed in the reactor compartment. The leak is in one control rod and we have initiated emergency shutdown of the reactor to a safe condition. There were no casualties or injuries."

"Engineering, bridge; isolate the leak and restore the reactor to operation," said Gallant.

"Bridge, engineering; Aye aye, sir. Estimated recovery within two hours."

Gallant hovered nearby as two workers squatted beneath the piping manifold applying patches.

They successfully isolate the leaking control rod and restarted the reactor.

Gallant called Walker to report to him on the bridge. Walker recommended that they operate the reactor at less than ninety per cent capacity for several days while he permanently repaired the damage. Gallant agreed.

They were fortunate that the accident occurred while they were near Base Kepler and could safely limp back to that haven while they affected repairs.

The journey to the base was mercifully uneventful.

Once there, they were able to complete repairs.

Gallant frowned when it was reported that the last routine maintenance on the rector control rods had not been performed. He wondered if he should take time from operations to sit at Base Kepler and catchup on maintenance and training before continuing missions into enemy territory.

The series of malfunctions was troubling and Gallant was at a loss of what he could do about them this far from a shipyard.

28

ALL IN

It didn't have the most comfortable chairs on the ship, but Gallant managed to spend the whole day sitting in CIC while he stared at the plunder he had stolen from the Titans. The loot consisted of many, many gigabits of data residing in a huge database. How many hours had he been studying the messages? He couldn't recall. He could have asked the CIC analysts who had undergone several watch shifts since he started, but why bother. It wouldn't give him any contentment. He swore to himself—intent on getting the job finished. He agonized over the translation and analysis of the stolen messages they had accumulated for two months. The ship's AI computer had run nonstop, all day, every day, applying correlation algorithms that the CIC techs had designed. The algorithms took the messages that Gallant had translated and linked missions, ships, commanders, and locations, in order to construct hypothetical scenarios for the related military orders—all calculated to yield actionable military intelligence.

There are eccentrics in all rates of the service, but the CIC analysts were an odd collection unto themselves. Under McCall's direction they used their problem-solving talents to dissect the data and extract possibilities.

Several of the CIC techs were sitting around the circular table with Gallant, McCall, Gabriel, and Clay. The diverse collection of grim expressions told a story of troubled dissention. They were all looking at the virtual screen of summarized data projected over the center of the table. The AI analyzer highlighted key components of the data. The room seemed hotter and stuffier than usual, but at least a refreshing breeze blew in through ventilation ducts.

"I don't doubt for a moment," said Gallant, "that this important puzzle must be resolved to a single conclusive solution and only that solution should be transmitted to Fleet Command."

"I disagree. You can't be sure of finding a definitive answer," said McCall.

"Well, commander, put yourself in the Titan's position. Would you send military fleet orders of such importance without the comprehensive goal of striking a fatal blow at the United Planets?"

"No, I wouldn't," said McCall.

No one who knew McCall could doubt that she would not risk her career on speculation.

"The Titans have been looking to exploit their current strategic position by unleashing a lethal attack on the inner planets," said Gallant, convinced of his argument.

"That may be likely," said McCall, reluctantly.

"And if they are prepared to attack soon then the many raids they have already sent to attack Mars must have been peremptory moves designed to test the UP responses under various scenarios. They have proven themselves to prefer highly involved multipronged attacks and our captured information fits that profile."

"Well . . .," said McCall showing irritation at being forced by logic into making a momentous decision, and one she did not want to be held accountable for, even as she continued to struggle against it.

"I meant no disrespect to your analysis. Of course you must decide where your duty lies," said Gallant, looking from her to Clay, and then back to her.

McCall said, "We have to solve this dilemma and I think, that with my guidance, we've made pretty good progress. I don't want to leave out the alternative scenarios when we send our report."

"You continue to refuse to reach a final conclusion."

McCall said, "When you try to solve an impenetrable problem, you must find resources in every element involved. There are always more layers than appear on the surface. This is a puzzle of fleet movements and deployments, and orders that must be made to mesh together into a coherent picture."

Gallant had reviewed the findings and the techs, likewise, had kept his translations accurate by repeatedly challenging his message interpretations. Together they discovered what appeared to be an imminent Titan war plan to attack Mars. It remained to convince McCall to transmit that conclusion to Fleet Command without a multitude of qualifying statements.

"Their plan uses a series of diversionary raids intended to splinter the UP fleet making Mars vulnerable to a powerful strike from the asteroids," summarizing his final assessment of the information.

"Let's go through this one more time. Convince me that this scenario represents the only possible truth—a truth, we can place the entire future of our people on," demanded McCall.

Gallant looked at her patiently.

Clay shifted uncomfortably in his chair. He appeared about to say something, but was uncertain how to intervene in an argument between senior officers.

Gabriel sat listening trying to absorb the arguments, but was already completely committed to his commanding officer.

The techs looked at one another waiting for orders.

McCall said, "An analyst should study all the information and assess each piece's relative merits along with its flaws. Once that's complete, he can formulate a prediction, or estimation. Analysts should never engage in fortunetelling."

"We can't use a fortuneteller," Gallant said, "but we could use a reliable prediction based upon the facts gathered and verified."

"That's the issue," she said. "We have to establish the validity of each message and weigh it against your translation and interpretation. We have lots of indirect information related to military operations from civilian and administrative sources, the details of which may, or may not, be factual. And we also have a few direct military sources. But how do we know they aren't deliberately planted, or wrong, or misleading, or subject to a different interpretation."

Gallant drummed his fingers on the table. He said, "We are operating under the assumption that the Titans don't know we can translate their military orders. So they have no need to create false trails for our intelligence service."

McCall responded, "They may not be planting false information for us. They could be trying to deceive their own population for propaganda purposes."

"Based on my impression of the interviews I've had with the prisoners, and the messages I've translated, I feel that population propaganda is an unlikely possibility," said Gallant.

McCall looked unmoved.

Gallant said, "We have the operational orders given directly to the Titan armada, squadron by squadron. In this case, the ability to look at a seemingly random set of events and identify an emerging pattern was achieved using our

AI computer. The pattern that emerged draws a graphic picture of fleet movements starting from the asteroid belt and striking at Mars, first with diversionary feints and then with one massive blow. We even have their high command's direct orders to several fleet commanders."

"I suggest we inform Mars headquarters about our conclusions about an attack, but include a discussion about the relative likelihood of alternative hypotheses, not just the most likely one."

"Given the time limitation and the fact that we can't transmit the entire database, it is up to us to provide our best scenario and stick with that. It would be unfair to ask them to second guess us and wade through a list of alternative scenarios. It would cause confusion, and worse, hesitation. We have been at this for two months; they can't duplicate our intimate understanding of the weight to give each bit of evidence. If we trust in our findings, we must recommend their adaption and rigorously defend them," said Gallant.

The discussion had started out calmly and professionally, but it was now becoming heated.

McCall continued to negotiate to leave the report as vague as possible to avoid any possibility of subsequent blame should the information prove false. She struggled to keep her personal feelings hidden.

Gabriel could see the byplay of the senior officers and remained silent.

There was a whirl of excitement around the table as the tension mounted. Gallant looked from face to face.

McCall was apparently seeking support for her arguments from Clay, but he was wavering. A glance at the tech showed they were uncertain.

Gallant wondered if he could offer a more persuasive argument.

"You've made some good points, commander," he said, "But I'm convinced that it would lead to procrastination on the part of Fleet Command and a lost opportunity of the United Planets."

"You are not dealing with this correctly, captain. We'll look like fools if these messages were garbled by your translation, or if our analysis proves faulty."

"This is not just a chance to avoid a beating from the Titans. It is an opportunity to turn the table on them. We wouldn't get another chance like this, maybe forever."

"It's too risky."

"Too risky for the fleet? Or too risky for your career?" asked Gallant pointedly.

Infuriated, McCall turned beet red.

"We need to transmit our report immediately," said Gallant, unwilling to temporize any further.

McCall didn't look like she could be made to yield.

McCall stood up and raised her fists over her head, she shouted, "No! You can't send those conclusions. I am responsible for the analysis of the data and I refuse to approve your conclusions."

All the men stood up in surprise.

She said ominously, "It's all too much about you! You acquired the information, you translated it, you analyzed it, and now you've reached the final conclusion," she pounded her fists on the table, "I don't believe a Natural is capable of playing so decisive a role in our survival. You will lead us all to disaster! It's all on your head."

Gallant composed himself and sat back down. He said calmly, "I'm willing to take full responsibility. It's the only way to ensure that Fleet Command will have faith in our conclusions and then take action. Collingsworth can still choose to not take it as credible, but at least this will be timely, targeted, and actionable. We can't send raw data and a plethora of diverse options. It's up to us to reach the best conclusions from what we've done. No one else can have the same assurance about what is real and what is wishful thinking."

Clay looked at Gallant then at McCall. His words surprised everyone, "I agree with the captain."

McCall looked as if she had been struck. She realized she had lost her main supporter and any further argument would be in vain.

Gallant offered her a face saving option. He said, "I will take full responsibility for the conclusions in the report, but I will allow you to write a short dissenting opinion that will be included in the transmission."

McCall said through gritted teeth, "Thank you."

An hour later the document was ready for transmission.

Gallant leaned forward and reviewed the material one more time before signing it. He wondered if Fleet Command would be able to read between the lines and realize how much of the report was guess work and how much was logical deduction.

It was time to send the report.

A chime rang indicating the OOD wanted to speak to the captain. Gallant tapped his comm pin and asked, "Yes?"

"Sir, we're ready to begin transmission."

Gallant pictured McCall's sour face as he said, "Commence transmitting."

The report was encrypted and fed through an AI system into a directional laser aimed at Mars. It wouldn't arrive for many hours.

Gallant thought,

I have to believe in myself, even if no one else does.

29

TRAP

A great weight had been lifted from Gallant's shoulders. He had spied, intrigued, and probed the enemy's domain. He had discovered actionable intelligence of a pending Titan attack, and he had submitted a detailed report to his superiors. It was now up to them to decide if they believed the intelligence, his report, and him. They could change fleet deployments, movements, and orders—if they chose to trust the intelligence. If they disbelieved the report in part or in whole, they might take little or no action. He'd done his job. What more could he do?

Sure, he could continue to monitor communications and be alert for additional information and any changes in Titan plans. He could continue to conduct sabotage operations and anything that might disrupt the enemy. But that was for another day. For today, he didn't have anything planned. The *Warrior* was recharging her battery at Base Kepler, and he was lying on his cot in his cabin being deliciously lazy.

Yes, lazy. Why not? I've earned it!

He closed his eyes and let his mind drift. It found its way to another world, another time. He fell into a twilight half-sleep and, in that dim reality, he recalled a beautiful young woman he still longed for—Aliana. He dreamed of all the things he could be doing that had nothing to do with war, battle, or death. He longed for the peace and comfort that existed on a planet far, far away . . .

BANG! BANG!

There was a loud banging on his cabin door.
"Captain?"

BANG! BANG!

"Captain?"
Gallant petulantly ignored the interruption and tried to recapture the bliss he was being dragged away from.

BANG! BANG!

"Captain, sir?"
No escape.
"Enter," he said.
A communication tech opened a crack in the door and stuck his head in. He mumbled, "The officer of the deck sends his respects, sir. He's sorry to disturb you, but we're receiving a broadcast from Fleet Command."

"Very, well." Gallant was up and out the door before the tech could move out of his way. The man fell back against the bulkhead as Gallant scampered up the dozen steps to the bridge.

"Captain on the bridge," said the OOD.

"At ease. Report," said Gallant to Roberts, who was standing by the communications console.

"We're receiving an encrypted broadcast from Fleet Command, sir. It was transmitted several hours ago using a wide directional beam aimed at Saturn in general. It's pretty garbled, but we've managed to decipher it."

It was barely two days since Gallant had transmitted the report—he hadn't expected an acknowledgment, or a decision, so soon. They had laid out their hypothesis; now came the moment of truth. There were tense faces on the bridge.

Gallant examined the message tablet.

REPORT ACCEPTED.

REQUIRE EXACT ATTACK TIMETABLE AND FLIGHT PATH OF ENEMY FLEET.

COLLINGSWORTH.

That's Collingsworth, thought Gallant, *decisive.*

"Apparently, Fleet Command has decided to act on our report, sir," said Roberts.

Gallant nodded.

Thanks to the *Warrior's* report, Fleet Command would set up an ambush for the Titans and beat them before they could begin a nuclear bombardment. The Titans' plan called for hundreds of cruisers and destroyers to conduct a series of raids on all inner planets to divert UP strength, starting in about ten days. This was to be followed by a full-strength attack by the armada coming from Ceres straight at Mars. Gallant sent details of the armada's strength and composition. He had recommended that Fleet Command keep its main fleet together at Mars and ignore the raiders, leaving local forces to defend the planets.

Based upon this information, there was an obvious counterstrategy. If Fleet Command let local forces defend each planet against raiders, then it could keep the bulk of the fleet together, hidden behind the radar shadow of Mars. When the armada made its thrust, the UP fleet could surprise it. But for the surprise to succeed, the high command needed the exact flight path and timetable of the armada's attack. That information was kept secret by the Titans, and Gallant hadn't uncovered those details, as yet.

Gallant stared once more at the message . . .

REQUIRE EXACT ATTACK TIMETABLE AND FLIGHT PATH OF ENEMY FLEET.

He took a deep breath,
How do I do that?

30

IN HARM'S WAY

The report Gallant sent to Mars headquarters contained detailed information about the upcoming Titan plan of attack. Their plan was based upon a series of diversionary raids intended to splinter the UP fleet. Once a large portion of the fleet was occupied chasing raiders, the Titan armada would emerge from the asteroid belt, starting at Ceres, and head straight for Mars with the intention of destroying the remaining defenders before the UP fleet could reassemble there.

Fleet command's counter strategy was to let local forces defend each planet against raiders, and keep the bulk of the fleet together, hidden behind the radar shadow of Mars for a surprise attack. But for the surprise to succeed, the high command needed the exact flight path and timetable of the armada's attack.

Gallant realized it was up to him to secure the remaining critical data. But it wasn't going to be easy. He conceived a plan to penetrate the alien's military headquarters on Pandora, where he was sure the flight path and timetable data must reside. He planned to first recover the recording device he had left on that moon during his last visit, but that would probably not have all the information he needed. He would expand his collection efforts to include the Titans' fleet headquarters and steal the data directly from their high command AI computer system. He thought about attempting the mission alone since such a bold undertaking would have only a slight chance of success. He grimaced momentarily as dread and self-doubt flowed through his mind. The truth was that he was afraid—not of pain or death, but of failure. Failure would mean the deaths of millions.

I can't do this without Gabriel. If this has any chance to succeed, I'll need his help.

It was at this moment that Admiral Collingsworth's words sprang back into his mind, "You will put your closest comrades into the greatest danger."

The memory hit him like a cold bucket of water. Right then he decided to take as much of the burden upon himself as possible.

He moved to his desk and activated his computer console. He called up the detailed schematics and maps of Pandora and its facilities that his crew had meticulously compiled over the course of the last month. He traced out an orbit for Gabriel to maintain in the Wasp while he performed an EVA to the moon. He identified a deep, well-hidden cave where he could stash his EVA and battle armor while he trekked to the target building in camouflaged pressure suit. He smiled when he worked out a path that avoided most of the guard towers and sentries. His plan was only possible because of the incredible volume of detailed information his CIC had amassed. He calculated the minimum oxygen he would need to carry. He itemized the other equipment he would require, including explosive charges. He intended to plant explosives to sabotage a portion of the military headquarters as he left. This would throw off suspicion that he stole valuable intelligence. He hoped the Titans would assume he was on a straightforward sabotage operation similar to what had been launched around Jupiter. That way, his mission wouldn't tempt the Titans to change their attack plans.

It was going to be tight, but he began to believe he could carry it off.

He called Roberts into his cabin and outlined the plan.

"The chances of success . . ." said Roberts, shaking his head, letting his voice diminish into an embarrassing silence.

"Successful men don't give up, Mr. Roberts; that's what makes them successful," said Gallant.

Roberts nodded, but his face was ashen.

"Mr. Roberts, under no circumstances are you to endanger the *Warrior* by attempting to rescue us if we are captured or if the Wasp is crippled. If we succeed, we will transmit the critical data to you. That information is worth all our lives. It's your job to ensure it is retransmitted to Mars via our relay stations. Remember, that is your first and only priority."

Gallant paused and looked directly at his executive officer: "If we're killed or captured, it means we've failed. There will be nothing more to be gained by sacrificing the *Warrior* in a vain attempt to change that. Under those circumstances, you are to withdraw and return to Mars."

Roberts remained silent.

Gallant glared at his executive officer. "Is that clear?"

"Yes, sir," said Roberts, "crystal clear."

Gallant offered his hand, and Roberts shook it before saying with obvious sincerity, "Good luck, Henry."

"Thank you, John."

They rose and left the captain's cabin. Roberts moved to the bridge while Gallant went to the hangar bay. He passed a few uneasy minutes before strapping in and checking the ship's readiness for launch.

When Gabriel arrived and boarded the small craft, Chief Howard said, "Godspeed."

Gabriel responded in kind, and then he gave a funny little wave as if he were bidding a final farewell.

Gallant requested permission to take-off.

When the bridge approved, they launched the Wasp.

The *Warrior* remained in stealth mode outside the harbor while the Wasp made the long perilous descent down toward Pandora, surrounded by rocks and satellites. The two ships were now separated by several million kilometers.

The Wasp disguised its wake by following a cargo ship past the entrance channel through the rings and into the inner region close to the moon. They had planted a bug and recorders on this moon during previous missions. Now they intended to collect that information and steal more from the military headquarters.

Gabriel maneuvered the Wasp into a low orbit around the moon. When the Wasp pierced the thin atmosphere, the hull creaked from the strain. Buffeted by the violent winds of the atmospheric gases, the ship's metal fabric produced a vibrating noise that drowned out the ship's normal sounds. Gabriel picked out the landmarks and identified the key alien facilities. When he found the site he was looking for he placed the Wasp in geosynchronous orbit over the area.

For this mission, Gabriel would stay aboard the Wasp while Gallant used a jetpack to drop down to the surface.

Gallant reviewed his plan with the midshipman. "Gabriel, the small transmitter I'm taking to the surface has limited range, so wait for the data. As soon as you receive it, retransmit it to the *Warrior*. Once that's done, signal me and I will use my EVA suit to launch from the surface and achieve orbit. You can pick me up then. Do you understand?"

"Yes, sir."

The success of the mission was all about relaying information from Gallant to the Wasp, from the Wasp to the *Warrior*, from the *Warrior* to the Saturn relay station and then on to Mars command. Like dominos, everything had to fall in succession for the mission to succeed.

The Wasp proceeded to an orbit nearly over the alien headquarters building complex and Gallant exited the Wasp. Using his battle armor EVA suit with its jetpack he flew, or rather fell, to the moon's surface. He twisted and dove, gliding straight over volcanic activity and past granite mountains. He imagined his arms were wings reaching toward the surface. Flying like that was a thrill, and he was disappointed when it was over so soon.

He touched down several kilometers from the headquarters building where the volcanic islands of circular cones protruded from the rough rocky terrain. The landing area was in a valley with a volcanic river of lava flowing over the irregular surface and past a deep, narrow cave on the edge of a plateau that rose several hundred meters from the surface. The cave appeared to be the perfect hiding place for Gallant to stow his battle armor and equipment.

"I think I can see plumes of ash over the horizon, sir," radioed Gabriel.

Gallant saw a gray flash. "Yes, there's an ash cloud. I can use that for cover."

He stripped off his battle armor with its EVA jetpack and radio transmitter. That left him in a flimsy camouflage pressure suit with a breathing apparatus that held a limited oxygen supply. The suit gave him superior flexibility to move while he tried to remain hidden, but he would have only his handgun and personal combat skills as weapons. When his mission was completed and he had made it back to the cave, he would be able to don his battle armor and use its small transmitter to send the data to the Wasp.

Gallant stopped and considered his position. As he reached a ridge which was considerably exposed, there was motion to his right. There were several Titans patrolling, silhouetted by the planet's volcanic backdrop. He crawled back to the cave until the area was clear.

Gallant stacked an extra oxygen tank, food, and water supplies in a container in the back of the cave. After resting for what seemed like a long time but only a few minutes in reality, he made his way from the cave entrance. He carried an extra oxygen bottle under his camouflage gear. He set off. Luckily, the rocky surface was not too great an impediment, and the larger boulders offered some concealment. He walked, or more correctly, bounced in the low gravity for about twenty minutes over the jagged and irregular surface. It was a long hard climb despite the low gravity. The irregular toughness of the dispersed rocks slowed his travel. The starlight offered the only illumination as he picked his way. He proceeded through a gully and into a shallow depression with easy slopes along the sides. As he plodded ahead he was glad for the cover the slopes afforded. He planned on retracing his path after he completed his task.

He was sufficiently concealed when he approached the area close to the headquarter facility. The buildings of this complex were dome-shaped with opaque walls and no windows. The domes were nested in clusters of three and each had several oval doors that open by a simple touch. Gallant had timed his operation so that he would arrive when the military staff was at their sleep period. He dug a small hole to hide in while he waited and observed the guards on patrol. Although he was not weary, he was tense, so he rested until he saw an opportunity to plunge ahead.

He started to imagine the process he would go through to get inside the building. It would take patience and guile. There were armed guards passing near the entrance. He monitored the nearby guards' movements looking for an opportunity to run the gauntlet. Alternating between confidence and doubt, he decided to make his move. He sprang from his concealment to penetrate the headquarters building itself.

The building extended underground, but the aboveground portion had several observation towers and three visible entrances. At each corner of the structure was a small guard station. Gallant moved between several smaller buildings and avoided the sentries. He reached the entrance furthest from the observation tower and he was careful enough to avoid the area's simple security procedures. Video and electronic surveillance would not easily see past his camouflage gear, but he was concerned about his limited oxygen supply.

When he reached the oval hatch, he touched it and it cycled open leading into the airlock. There was no alarm as he entered the slight methane atmosphere within. In the first circular room he found a pair of large computers operating unattended. Although the tomblike room was not large, it took him a minute to find the door to the next room. He slipped inside and worked his way to what he assumed was the fleet commander's office with the main AI computer.

Using guesswork as much as anything, he made it inside. He activated the AI computer and connected a neural interface he had brought with him. He searched through the information, stretching his ability to translate the messages as quickly as possible. Overwhelming doubt crept into his mind. Nevertheless, he worked on, message after message, file after file. He queried the AI for assistance, but his requests were rejected as illogical. He concentrated and reformulated his request again. This time the AI offered him access to what he assumed was the supreme fleet commander's files.

Gotcha!"

Gallant found the secret stash of data--fulfilling his greatest hope. The discovery was sweet, but it did nothing to relieve his tension as reaction set in from the dangers around him. He took several moments to compose himself while his conscious nagged at him for squandering precious seconds.

Secrets are only prized if you can steal them in secret. So once he had collected everything he thought was of value, he set about disguising the fact that anything had been taken. He covered his computer tracks and erased all trace of his intrusive presence. He left the fleet commander's office and returned to the room where he had entered the building when . . .

BAM!

The sound startled him. It was not clear what made the noise, but it told him that he needed to get moving. Alone in the dark, he sensed that things were closing in on him. He sprang out the exit and began running. Once he was in the open courtyard, he began moving cautiously to avoid the tower lookouts and roving guards.

Motion in the corner of his eye alerted him. The hair on the back of his neck stood up. He sensed someone watching him, someone dangerous, someone close. He trusted his senses, but he resisted the temptation to look behind him. Instead, he threw himself flat to the ground. A guard walked by searching for intruders. Gallant sprang up and grabbed the guard from behind and twisted his neck. The crack told him that his enemy was finished.

He moved to a nearby building and planted explosive charge. He set it to go off in twenty minutes. That would lead them to believe that his mission was merely sabotage.

As he was leaving, several guards saw him and attacked. He grabbed the first one and threw him into the second. He then sidestepped the third, tripping him as he passed. He hit the first man with the butt of his palm as he tried to get up and then pushed him to one side. Gallant ducked the swinging rifle butt of one guard and punched him in his midsection, doubling him over and producing a distinct sound of escaping gases.

The first guard recovered, stepped forward, and swung a heavy object, Gallant avoided the blow--grabbed the guard's wrist and twisted it until he dropped the weapon.

The remaining guard, a large beefy fellow, charged Gallant like a raging bull. He wrapped his arms around

Gallant and wrestled him to the ground whereupon all three guards began hitting and kicking him.

The blows were telling and Gallant struck back in desperation.

He thought,

They're playing for keeps.

Pain grabbed him as they punched and kicked him. Gallant put his faith in his hand-to-hand combat training. He twisted his body and grabbed one guard's arm for leverage—allowing him to get back on his feet.

With one hand, Gallant chopped the forearm of the first guard, breaking it—taking him out of the fight. Then he kicked the kneecap of the second guard—breaking it as well.

The third guard hit Gallant in the jaw, snapping his head back. He shook off the pain and used the flat of his right hand to chop the guard's exposed throat, but he failed to connect solidly. Gallant blocked another punch with his left forearm and delivered a devastating right-cross shattering the guard's face and sending blood flying in all directions.

The guards, panting—grimacing in pain—remained on the ground. They had had enough.

Gallant fled from the area.

Once he was away from the buildings and making his way through the ravines, a guard began shooting in his general direction. He tried to head to the cave, but the shooting forced him to move slower than he wanted.

He sought cover within the topsy-turvy combat environment even as his pursuers sought him.

Damn! This is going to be a test of wills, he thought.

Gallant crawled forward and crouched in a trench. He let loose a few shots at a Titan in the most exposed position. He then charged straight at a second group of three exposed aliens. Heroics were a good way to get killed, but his training paid off as he dispatched the enemy.

About sixty meters away, there were several Titans. They ducked after Gallant fired. When he reached the end of the ledge, he fired again. He thought there were several more ahead, and he crawled forward to get them. Throwing grenades, he crept forward, making for the cover behind mounds of volcanic rock. The unnerving dark was finally broken by a series of bright noisy explosions. He then withdrew.

The explosive charges he had set twenty minutes earlier finally went off with a satisfying bright detonation. It marked his time to escape. He saw plasma weapons shriek into the dark and leave a smoldering display of fireworks. There was another explosion, but he didn't know who had set it off. Perhaps the Titans were using heavy weapons. The brilliant flashes of plasma weapons shrieked past him and struck a nearby rock.

What's happening?

His sight slowly returned, leaving a glare in his eyes. The attackers had no idea where he was hiding, but were laying down suppressing fire to flush him out as they moved forward. Breathlessly, he shrank behind a bolder.

It was not long before the clamor attracted more attention.

The dark swooping shadows cast by the guards wheeled toward him. He was aware of a threat to his left. It was a guard carrying a plasma rifle illuminated in a search light. Gallant didn't wait for the onslaught, but rose to meet it firing as rapidly as he could. The clash of their meeting was beset by white fury and burning hot plasma. The searchlight went dark as a great shadow descended like a falling cloud. A shot splashed against the stones.

That was all he could discern from his brief look. He went forward, swinging his gun from side to side. Any time he detected a flicker of motion, he aimed the gun in that direction. As he leveled his weapon, he noticed the presence of several more aliens.

With all the bravado he could muster, he thrust himself forward, firing, and killing the aliens in succession. He shook with excitement, even though the well-trained part of him responded logically by reminding him to remain calm. He thrust the images of the dead bodies out of his mind, along with the heavy thoughts that accompanied them.

Another alien appeared out the dark and fired a handgun at him. The plasma blast grazed Gallant's left arm, causing him to slip and stumbled with a cry of bitter pain.

As his suit automatically resealed itself, Gallant returned fire, and the face of the alien dissolved into a bloody mess.

He recognized that at this point, he didn't have any good options.

Firing back at vague figures in the dark, he got up and ran at breakneck speed in the low gravity. He fired his plasma handgun at the aliens. They tossed a grenade, and the flash of light gave him a chance to get his bearings. Looking away, he lost his footing, bounced up, and sprawled back down across the ground. Rebounding, he continued to retreat toward his sanctuary, the cave. The nearby blinding flashes of plasma weapons again streaked past him and left a smoldering display of fireworks as they ricocheted off the rocks.

Gallant ran, gasping for breath as his oxygen supply dwindled. He hoped to reach the cave. Peering over his shoulder, he tripped on a jagged rock and crashed to the ground. He lay still, taking inventory of the pain as he groaned softly. A sudden wave of nausea swept over him. He had to move and move quickly, but before he could do so, a laser shot struck him in the side, penetrating his pressure suit. The suit began losing precious oxygen until the automatic self-sealant closed the leak.

How much oxygen is left?

His body was traumatized and a sickening sense of defeat grabbed him, causing multiple convulsive stomach spasms. He vomited blood from the internal wound. The revolting, sticky red fluid spewed out into his mouthpiece. He struggled to tap down the growing panic when he couldn't catch his breath.

He revived his inner resolve and slowly gathered his strength. He forced himself to rise and resume running. He bounced along the surface and finally found the cave where he had left his equipment.

He donned his battle armor and let its automatic medical sensors activate. He sucked medication and stimulants from the fluid-dispensing straw within his helmet and then bit his lip from the searing pain. He tried to keep himself alert to prevent succumbing to shock. He felt needles enter his flesh and pump analgesics and plasma into him. He flipped on his high magnification thermal lens and took a good look around. At the same time, he used the suit's transmitter to begin sending the data to the Wasp in orbit high above. He was tempted to order Gabriel to leave without him, but he decided he would only do that as a last resort.

After what seemed an eternity, Gabriel reported that he had received the data, but he was unable to raise the *Warrior* at the current distance.

Gallant asked him to try again. Again the transmission failed.

Gallant saw a guard approach the entrance to the cave. The guard began shooting, but his laser beam bounced harmlessly off Gallant's armor. He returned fire. Then the guard got a lucky shot that struck Gallant's jetpack, producing a prodigious hole and causing a jet stream of leaking gases that drained the fuel supply in seconds.

Gallant exchanged several more shots with the lone guard until he finally hit him. The guard fell lifelessly to the ground.

Gallant examined the wrecked jetpack. He wasn't going to be able to patch it. His mind searched through a mass of options for a means of escape. There were none. He was trapped. There was no choice now. He wasn't going anywhere.

Another guard closed in on the cave entrance. He shot the guard, but he knew others would follow. His oxygen was running low and everything was spinning around him. He sighed a deep sigh.

He used his small EVA suit transmitter and ordered, "Gabriel, I must speak to you plainly because there is no room for debate. Listen and obey my orders exactly. Do you understand?"

"Yes, sir."

"We are in a perilous situation. My EVA is damaged, and I can't take off from the moon. If we work together, rapidly and resolutely, we can still complete our mission. But the chances of one or both of us surviving are small indeed."

Gallant was sickened by the words he was now forced to speak, "Gabriel, this data must get through no matter what—even if it kills me—even if it kills you. Resolve yourself to that, and fight like you never thought possible."

"I will, sir."

"Try transmitting the data one more time."

Gabriel tried again to transmit the data, but again he failed. His transmitter was not powerful enough to bridge the distance.

"No go, sir."

"OK, that's it. I'm ordering you to leave me and head for the *Warrior*. Transmit the data continuously until you get through. When you reach the ship, you are to dock and make no attempt to rescue me. The *Warrior* is to exit the area. Is that clear?"

"Sir?"

"I asked if that was clear," said Gallant as forcefully as he could manage.

"Yes, sir."

Gallant added softly, "Go. It's all right. Go."

Gallant monitored his radio as the Wasp departed orbit and streaked away from Pandora.

The Wasp flew toward its mother ship, all the while transmitting the crucial data and waiting for an acknowledgement.

But the only signal Gallant heard over the radio was, "Captain, the Wasp is experiencing harmonic fluctuations again. I can't control it."

Gallant realized that the strain of flying the Wasp while maintaining the stealth containment field was proving too difficult under the stressful circumstance and when an anomaly appeared in the harmonic frequency, Gabriel had a problem keeping it in eurythmic balance.

"I'm using my neural interface to try and restore the power imbalance, but the stealth field is acting up and I'm losing power. The ship is becoming exposed as the cloaking field dims."

A nearby Titan destroyer picked up traces of the Wasp and began firing its lasers at the unexpected target.

The fragile ship was hit and crippled—for the young midshipman, it was as if the heavens had fallen down upon him. There was no sensation of the damage itself, but air leaked from the ship.

"I have a hull rupture!" Gabriel's panicked voice blared over the radio.

"What's happening?" asked Gallant.

The destroyer fired and hit the Wasp again.

"I've been wounded," came over the radio.

Gallant pictured the midshipman's youthful face disfigured, splattered with blood.

More explosions continued to reverberate against the hull of the Wasp. This wasn't a time for poor choices. One mistake could be his last. Gabriel reported that he was attempting to patch a major leak. He worked with energy trying to clear away the wreckage, but the loss of oxygen was disconcerting.

Gallant waited for each precious radio message explaining Gabriel's situation, but time was a thief taking precious options away.

Finally, Gabriel said, "I got through! The *Warrior* acknowledged receipt of the data! They got it!"

Gallant breathed a sigh of relief. He wanted to be happy at the news, but he was wounded and marooned on Pandora, and Gabriel was wounded and under attack in the Wasp.

Gabriel radioed, "I can't control the power to the stealth field and operate the damaged ship. The destroyer is launching a spread of missiles. I can't cloak the ship. I'm defenseless."

A minute later, Gallant could make out a bright flash overhead that could only be the *coup de grace* for the Wasp—and the death of Michael Gabriel.

An unbearable sorrow poured over Gallant.

31

BAND OF BROTHERS

Gallant was uncertain how much time had passed while he lay on the ground bleeding in his battle armor, lost in thought,

Someone has to fight, but during combat—inevitably—somebody dies. You hope it isn't you, but when it happens to your shipmate, that's painful, too. You carry on, but you question yourself. You force yourself to believe that that death mattered.

Wounded and stranded on Pandora, death was also waiting for him. He selfishly thought about his pain and his predicament until, finally, he found acceptance. It was better to lie still and wait than agitate over something he could not change. So he closed his eyes and waited for oblivion—it didn't come. But with absolutely stunning clarity, he understood that he had failed both Gabriel and himself. The distress of his failure hit home with a vengeance. He had experienced loss before, but the depth of his sorrow over the death of his young charge humbled him. He should've foreseen that outcome—he had not. The only saving grace was that the vital information had been sent to the *Warrior,* and she was safe.

He cherished that thought and found it comforting until, to his utter astonishment, he picked up another radio transmission.

"Gallant . . . Come in . . . Gallant. Report your location." *What? Who?*

"Gallant, this is Clay. I'm in the Hummingbird in orbit over Pandora. I need your exact location."

His illusion of the *Warrior's* safety shattered, Gallant switched on his homing beacon. Dazed and shaken, he struggled to his feet.

"Damn it, Clay! What are you doing here?"

"Roberts decided we should come and get you. The *Warrior* entered orbit in stealth mode, and I flew the Hummingbird to Pandora looking for you."

"The Hummingbird is a single-seat craft with no stealth capability. Only a complete fool, or a suicidal maniac, would try to reach me."

"At your service, sir," said Clay with a flamboyant flare. "I've stripped the craft bare. I should be able to squeeze you in." Clay's plan was unprecedented and, obviously, had been devised on the spur of the moment. Nevertheless, he was known as a man of original ideas, not to mention unbridled courage.

It was difficult to overestimate the danger Clay had placed himself in. He had flown an exposed, unarmed small craft into the middle of an enemy stronghold. He was over a heavily fortified moon filled with sensor arrays and missile batteries. There were numerous patrol ships in the area and heavily armed cruisers. The flippant attitude he displayed only served to heighten Gallant's concern.

"What about the data?" Gallant asked.

"Gabe passed it to us before the Wasp was destroyed. We relayed the data to Base Kepler for retransmission to Mars," said Clay. "We've done our job. Our mission is complete. All that's left is to collect our misplaced skipper."

"I failed Gabriel," confessed Gallant.

"Save your soul searching until we get back."

Gallant said, "I specifically ordered Roberts not to hazard the *Warrior* in a rescue attempt."

Clay offered his unorthodox advice: "Life occasionally gives you a second chance, skipper. Just live with it."

Gallant brooded until he saw the Hummingbird slip over the horizon, clear evidence that Clay had the courage of his convictions.

"I've got a fix on you, skipper. I'll be there in two minutes. Be ready to move quickly."

When the Hummingbird touched down, Gallant scampered toward it. An alien opened fire with a plasma rifle from several hundred meters away. Gallant clambered aboard the small craft, stripped off his battle armor, and threw it from the ship. Hastily he reached for a first aid kit and searched for a bandage.

Clay wasted no time in taking off and climbing into space fully aware that Titan patrol ships would soon be after them. They raced toward the *Warrior*, but the exposed

Hummingbird was immediately spotted by the same destroyer that had dispatched the Wasp. The alien ship turned on an intercepting course, but so did the *Warrior*.

"You've given that destroyer a good point to aim at," Gallant said. "Let's hope he takes his time before shooting."

As the destroyer closed on the Hummingbird, the *Warrior* silently crept up on the destroyer.

"Sound general quarters!" the OOD ordered.

The weapons batteries were ready with nervous fingers on the trigger when Roberts dropped the *Warrior's* stealth cloak. They drew a bead on the enemy and fired the ship's FASER cannon directly at the destroyer's midsection. With unerring accuracy, the weapon team's aim was on target; the cannon scored a direct hit.

Ignoring the vulnerable Hummingbird, the destroyer retaliated by launching four missiles at the *Warrior*.

Gallant's eyes were blinded by the flash of the explosion. He blinked repeatedly as he tried to find his vision.

The *Warrior* hurled several antimissile missiles and deployed decoys. The sloop's countermeasures proved effective; none of the alien's missiles exploded close enough to do any real damage.

The wily destroyer then reversed course and began zigzagging as it prepared to let another salvo fly.

In desperation, the *Warrior* fired, but the Titan ship continued to attack. The adversaries exchanged several more shots before there was an explosion that seriously damaged the Titan ship. Everyone on board the *Warrior* was relieved when they saw the enemy ship change course and limp away. But several other enemy warships were now approaching the area, drawn to the conflict.

Clay brought the Hummingbird to the *Warrior* and docked inside the launch bay. As soon as the Hummingbird was secured, Roberts chose the prudent decision to seek shelter, and he ordered, "Engage stealth mode, full power."

"Aye aye, sir."

The *Warrior*'s cloaking containment field expanded and the ship disappeared from the enemy's view.

"Helm, return to base course. Get us out of here!" ordered Roberts.

"Aye aye, sir."

When Gallant reached the bridge, his first words were, "Roberts, I specifically ordered you not to attempt a rescue. Your duty was to safeguard the *Warrior* and our mission."

"Oh, hell, I never took that order seriously," said Roberts with a completely out-of-character grin.

"Why not?" asked Gallant flabbergasted.

"Because I didn't think there was a snowball's chance in hell we'd get away from Pandora alive," Roberts deadpanned.

Gallant could offer no rebuttal.

"Besides, I already transmitted the critical data to Base Kepler. Our mission was complete, so I felt free to make a command decision and make an attempt to pull you out," concluded Roberts, looking self-satisfied.

Gallant sunk into his command chair and let Roberts navigate the ship to safety. Soon they were well away from pursuing aliens and back at Base Kepler, recharging their stealth battery. They remained there quietly listening for the civilian communications being broadcast from Mars.

"The trouble with the spy business," Gallant said, "is that it's left to someone else to act. You're forced to wait unending hours to find out if your labors have paid off."

Roberts nodded.

It wasn't until ten days later that they were both gratified to hear the welcome broadcast from Mars. The entire crew listened in rapt attention as the announcement described a great battle that had been waged around Mars with this result:

"VICTORY! VICTORY!"

Surprise had been achieved—like all surprise was achieved in war—through surreptitious intelligence. The desperate gamble had paid off and the UP fleet—in a colossal feat of ingenuity, courage, and daring—had decisively defeated the Titan armada.

An insane roar of triumph erupted aboard the *Warrior*.

32

SEALED ORDERS

Seated in his cabin, Gallant was conscious of an internal struggle he could only identify as an abnormality in his thought process. After all this time, he had hoped some new possibility might come to mind to allow him to make peace with the mission's outcome. Once again, his mind began to review the calculations he had previously made under duress, as if he could somehow achieve a reconciliation of his desired outcome with the actual results—something that would change the past into something more to his liking.

Putting aside his self-doubt, he bent over to reach the locking mechanism on his safe. He pressed his thumb print onto the keypad. Opening the safe, he removed a locked package that had resided there for the entire mission.

He tapped his comm pin and said, "Bridge, ask the XO to come to my cabin."

"Aye aye, sir."

There was a knock on his door a minute later.

"Enter."

"You asked to see me, skipper?" said Roberts.

"Yes. I would like you to verify that the *Warrior* has fulfilled our requirements for phase one of our mission under our current orders." Gallant handed Roberts a tablet with the list of mission requirements.

It took Roberts several minutes to go through the list. When he was satisfied, he pressed his thumbprint onto the tablet, verifying the mission requirements. He handed the tablet back to Gallant.

"Is that all, sir?"

"One more thing; please verify the electronic lock on this package containing our sealed phase two orders."

Roberts examined the package, which had remained unopened until then. "All correct, skipper."

"Thank you," said Gallant.

Roberts waited a minute, hoping he could remain.

Unwilling to enter a discussion with anyone at the moment, Gallant said, "That's all."

Disappointed, Roberts replied, "Aye aye, sir," and left.

Gallant opened his new orders. A life-size holographic image of Admiral Collingsworth projected into the cabin, and an audio recording played. "Henry, I assume you've successfully completed phase one of your orders," Collingsworth said. "Congratulations!"

Gallant nodded absentmindedly.

The holographic image grinned from ear to ear as if it could see the gesture. Collingsworth then continued:

"First, the good news—I'm authorizing your field promotion to lieutenant commander immediately and changing your posting from captain pro tem to captain. I realize these recognitions come late, but I never doubted that you deserved them.

"Now for the not-so-good news: You're not coming home. Your sealed orders provide detailed instructions, but let me summarize them: I'm sending you to Gleise-581. Your exploits at Jupiter and Saturn were training for the more formidable task of penetrating the Titans' home planet. I wish I could give you more than warm wishes, but you already have my trust and respect. Good Luck!"

Gallant took it all in and remained quiet for a long, long time. Finally, he opened his message tablet and began a new page. He had put this task off for as long as he could. Now it was necessary to write the letter he dreaded . . .

> Mr. and Mrs. Gabriel,
>
> It is my sad duty to inform you of the death of your son, Midshipman Michael Gabriel, who made the ultimate sacrifice in defense of our people. You have my deepest sympathy on your loss.
>
> I served with your son during his deployment aboard the *Warrior*. He was a caring and compassionate young man as well as an excellent officer. He was always doing

something for someone else but never taking credit for it. Michael was respected and admired by his shipmates for his love of service and family. He was also a capable and dependable officer, and for that reason he was often called upon for special assignments.

Giving one's life for others is the highest act of selflessness, and your son's valor occurred on a perilous mission where his sacrifice saved countless others. You can take solace in knowing that he died defending the people he loved so dearly.

He was an inspiration to us all. I am proud to have served with him, and I will always keep him in my thoughts to remind me why I continue to fight.

In Deep Sorrow,

Henry Gallant

Lieutenant Commander Henry Gallant
Commanding Officer, UP *Warrior* SS 519

Printed in Great Britain
by Amazon